D1635335
Zed Storm has lived in Japan
for the past five years and is a
master of several martial arts.
He has a wolfhound called Max,
and in his spare
time plays the guitar
and competes in
triathlons. He likes to
read about history, space
exploration, and rare
animals and he came up
with the idea for Will Solvit
while camping
in a Siberian forest.
www.will-solvit.com

ATTENTION: ALL READERS!

Wherever you see something that looks like this, reach for your decoder. Holding it by the corner, place the centre of your decoder over the lines. Rotate it very slowly, look closely and a picture will appear.

Mystery solved!

AND THE MISSION OF MENACE

Parragon

Bath · New York · Singapore · Hong Kong · Cologne · Delhi · Melbourne

Written by Zed Storm
Creative concept and words by E. Hawken
Check out the website at www.will-solvit.com

First edition published by Parragon in 2010

Parragon
Queen Street House
4 Queen Street
Bath BA1 1HE, UK

ISBN 978-1-4075-8981-7

Printed in China

Please retain this information for future reference.

5...4...3...2...1... BLAST OFF!

Whooosh!

Really cool guy

You might need this sooner than you think...

MORSE CODE

A	.–	N	–.	0	–––––
B	–...	O	–––	1	.––––
C	–.–.	P	.––.	2	..–––
D	–..	Q	––.–	3	...––
E	.	R	.–.	4	....–
F	..–.	S	...	5	.....
G	––.	T	–	6	–....
H	....	U	..–	7	––...
I	..	V	...–	8	–––..
J	.–––	W	.––	9	––––.
K	–.–	X	–..–	FULL STOP	.–.–.–
L	.–..	Y	–.––	COMMA	––..––
M	––	Z	––..	QUESTION MARK	..––..

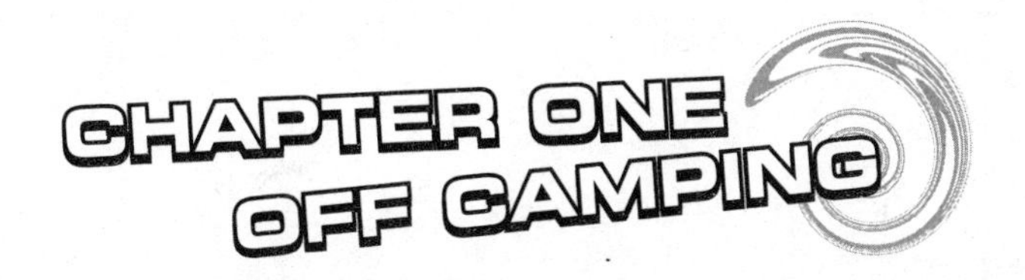

The best things in life never happen at school. So imagine my shock when my new teacher, Mrs Simmons, announced a few weeks ago that we were going on a class camping trip.

"And don't forget to pack your thermal underwear. It's cold this time of year!" she had warned us.

Now that time was here, and I jumped onto the school bus like a frog who'd stepped in itching powder.

In my opinion, camping's one of the best things you can do, except for playing on a games console. These are just a few of the reasons why I think camping is so cool:

- You get to sleep outside.
- You cook your food on a fire – like a caveman.
- There's a chance you might meet (and fight) a bear.
- You can camp anywhere: woods, tropical beaches, deserts, the Moon!

The drive to the campsite was soooo long and mega-boring. I avoided sitting next to Zoe by putting my bag on the seat next to me and pretending I was saving it for someone else. Zoe's a new friend, you see, and a girl. I don't usually do friendships with girls, but Zoe was sort of forced on me. I'd just started at a new school and didn't know anyone. At least she liked comics and football. She also happened to own some of the most impressive gadgets I'd ever seen – like her SurfM8 60 – a handheld Internet device with a GPRS modem so strong you could use it anywhere in the world!

Anyway, I'm racing ahead. I should introduce myself. I'm Will Solvit. I'm ten years old and I've been living with my Grandpa Monty ever since I lost my mum and dad in a dinosaur-infested jungle.

You think that sounds weird? I should probably explain. My dad's an inventor, and one day he had this bright idea to take us back in time in his machine, Morph. Morph can turn into anything you want it to be – space rocket, roller-coaster, helicopter, and in this case, a time machine. Anyway, to cut a long story short, I accidentally came home from that trip to the jungle without my parents, but with a T-rex instead! I haven't managed to get my parents back yet, although I haven't given up trying. Grandpa Monty keeps telling me that I should forget about it for now... that maybe Mum and Dad don't want to be rescued because Dad has important things to discover first. Anyway, that's a whole other story; I should get back to the camping trip.

I'd already thought ahead and turned Morph into an MP3 player for the drive, so I spent the whole journey listening to my favourite rock tunes and reading a comic book about sharks. Did you know that a shark's sense of smell is so incredible it can detect one drop of blood in a million drops of water? How's that for a frightening fact?

I started to pitch my tent as soon as I got off the bus. Once it was up, I climbed in and unpacked my bag. I took out my comic book, sleeping stuff, Morph, biscuits (in case I got hungry), and Dad's Supersonic Screecher, which I put in my pocket. (The Supersonic Screecher is an invention to scare off dangerous animals with its supersonic screeching noises. Dad used to pack it whenever he took me camping so we could scare off bears and lions.)

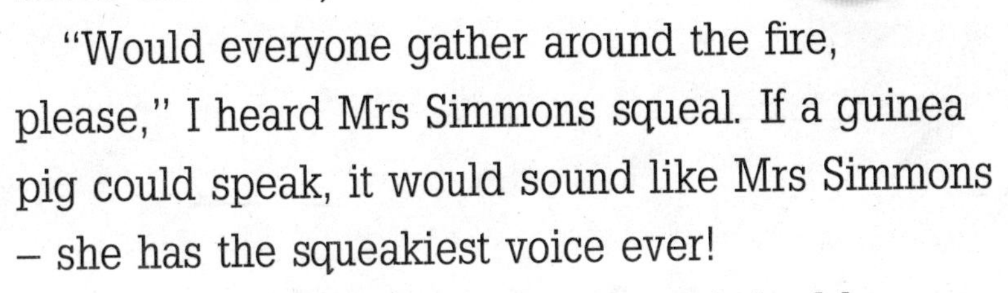

"Would everyone gather around the fire, please," I heard Mrs Simmons squeal. If a guinea pig could speak, it would sound like Mrs Simmons – she has the squeakiest voice ever!

"You should all have your tents pitched by now," Mrs Simmons yelped. "But we'll give you another half hour before we gather around the fire for soup and singing."

My mouth dropped open in shock.

Campfire singing = LAME.

"Those of you who already have your tents up

have some free time," Mrs Simmons said. "Please don't leave the campsite..."

Too late – I was off!

I wanted to explore. Goodbye teachers, hello adventure! I took my torch and slipped away so I could check out the woods around the campsite.

The ground was covered with leaves and smelled like compost. I could hear the flapping of wings overhead. I shone my torch into the trees above, hoping to find giant vampire bats, but I didn't see any. Instead, I saw a small white square perched between some branches.

From where I was standing, I could tell that it was an envelope, and I knew exactly the kind of envelopes that could be found somewhere as crazy as up a tree: envelopes with my name on them! They'd been sent to me before. They'd helped me find Grandpa Monty's secret – that he used to be a spy! They had also helped me find out that my dad, my grandpa, and every member of the Solvit family who lived before them had all been Adventurers, and that I was destined to be one too, although I still had to find out exactly what kind of Adventurer I would be.

I quickly looked around, just to check that no one had followed me. They hadn't; I was alone. Putting the torch in my pocket, I grabbed the lowest tree branch and pulled myself up. Then I began to scale the tree as quietly as I could. The letter was pretty high up, and I had to pull off some serious monkey moves to reach it.

I aimed my torch beam at the front of the envelope. It was just as I had expected.

I stuffed the envelope into my pocket and quickly climbed down the tree.

Back on the ground, I opened the letter.

WHEN DO ASTRONAUTS HAVE LUNCH?

AT LAUNCHTIME!

IT'S BEEN A WHILE SINCE I'VE WRITTEN TO YOU.
BY NOW YOU'VE HAD PLENTY OF TIME TO COME
TO TERMS WITH WHO YOU ARE AND THE LIFE
THAT YOU MUST LEAD.
BEING AN ADVENTURER ISN'T ALWAYS FUN.
IT WILL BRING GREAT RESPONSIBILITIES.
WE CAN NEVER KNOW WHAT THE FUTURE HOLDS,
BUT WE CAN PREPARE OURSELVES FOR ANYTHING.
LOOK TO THE SKIES.

- .... . | .--. .- .-. - . -.- | .- .-. . . | -.-.
--- -- .. -. --.

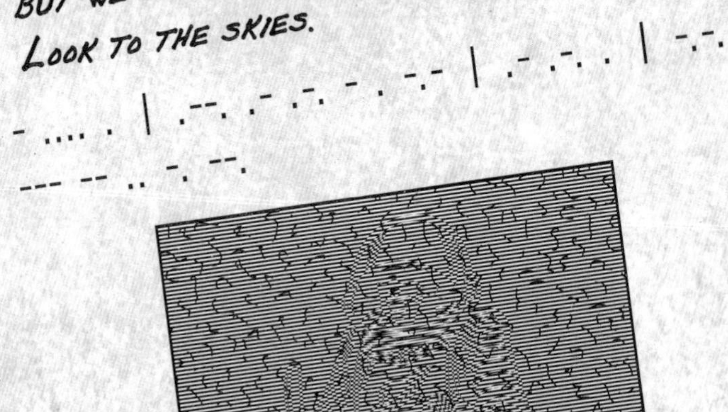

Adventurers have responsibilities? Look to the skies? What did that mean?

Letters always left me with so many questions. But the thing that bothered me most was the marks at the bottom of the letter. I knew exactly what they were – Morse code. I'd seen it in Grandpa's spy diary. But why was it being used in my letter? What was so secret that it had to be written in code?

I needed to know what the message meant as soon as possible, and the fastest way to translate it had to be the Internet. Morph had an Internet program, but I knew for a fact it wouldn't work in a campsite.

I needed a SurfM8 60, and I only knew one person who had something like that – and she was the last person in the cosmos that I wanted to ask for help.

CHAPTER TWO
CLOSE ENCOUNTERS

"Will Solvit!" someone screamed. Mrs Simmons!

I sprinted out of the woods towards the campsite as quickly as I could, and ran straight into Zoe.

"Found him!" Zoe shouted. "What's that?" she asked me, noticing the letter in my hand.

Zoe's quicker than a shark swimming towards fresh meat when it comes to noticing things – it drives me nuts. I quickly stuffed the letter into my pocket.

"Nothing," I said, trying not to sound like I was bluffing.

"Yeah, right," Zoe said. "If you want dinner you have to come back to the campsite."

My stomach suddenly made a really loud growling sound. I was pretty hungry.

"Zoe?" I asked. "Any chance I could borrow your SurfM8 60 for a few minutes?"

"Sure," she said, "if you let me hang out with you while you're using it."

"Fine," I groaned. I didn't exactly have a choice, did I?

We got to the campfire and Mrs Simmons passed me a cup of warm soup. I sat down by the fire to eat. If there's anything worse than the sound of Mrs Simmons's voice, then it's the sight of her. She looks like a giant troll who got dressed in the dark and has a family of birds nesting in her hair.

The singing session after dinner was pretty bad too. Mrs Simmons sounded like a dying cat and the other kids sounded like a troop of baboons

Mrs Simmons
Gee Gee!

with stomach aches. I thought my eardrums were going to burst!

After the torture had ended, Zoe went to get her SurfM8 60 and I walked towards the woods again.

Zoe ran to catch up with me.

"Where are we going?" she asked.

"Into the woods," I replied.

For a split second, I thought Zoe was going to get scared and chicken out. But she marched straight ahead of me.

I heard the leaves on the ground rustle. Three tabby cats suddenly darted between my legs, running farther into the trees. Strange, I thought. Since when do cats appear in woods?

"Can we just hang out here?" Zoe said, plonking herself down on a fallen tree branch. "I think we're far enough from camp. You know, I love camping. My dad used to take me all the time. One time, when I lived in Singapore, we stayed in the jungle overnight."

"Cool," I muttered. It reminded me of the last time I was in a jungle – it was where I lost Mum and Dad. Thinking about them makes me wish they were still here.

"How's your grandpa?" Zoe asked.

"I agreed to hang out. I didn't agree to talk about my family," I snapped at her.

Sometimes I think it would be good to talk about my parents. But I can't trust anyone with my secret. Besides, sometimes lies are more believable than the truth – especially when time travel is concerned.

"So why don't you want to talk about your family?" Zoe asked quietly. "What are you hiding?"

"Nothing!" I said loudly. "I don't ask you about

your family."

"You can if you want... I'll tell you anything you want to know. It's not very exciting. My parents are divorced. Dad still lives in Singapore, but Mum and I moved back here. I don't have any brothers or sisters. And that's about it, really."

I was half listening to Zoe and half thinking about stuff when I looked up at the sky. It was full of stars. It's cool that each star in the sky is like our sun. If the Sun has eight planets orbiting it, imagine how many planets spin around other stars!

"What were you thinking about?" asked Zoe.

"Nothing," I told her.

She made a huffing sound.

"Can I borrow your SurfM8 60 now, please?" I asked nicely.

"OK," she said slowly.

Wicked! She passed me the device and I switched it on. It didn't take me long to find a site that translated Morse code. I took the letter out of my pocket and carefully unfolded it. My gaze flicked up and I caught Zoe leaning over my shoulder and staring at the SurfM8 screen.

"Do you mind?" I said, annoyed. "This is private."

"Then get your own SurfM8 60," she snapped. "Why do you need to know about Morse code, anyway?"

"I want to teach myself how to use it," I lied.

I tapped the Morse code symbols into the small handheld gadget, making sure Zoe couldn't see what I was tapping in.

It only took a few seconds for the Internet to give a translation: **The Partek are coming.**

Who were the Partek? Why were they coming?

Out of nowhere, blinding lights suddenly flashed down from the sky.
Some kind of weird-shaped aircraft hovered above the trees, shining lights into the woods.
What's going on?
I don't know!
I handed the SurfM8 60 back to Zoe and ran off to investigate.
Zoe followed me through the woods.

Several hundred cats were gathered in a clearing, howling excitedly under the lights of the strange aircraft.

As we arrived, the lights vanished and the aircraft zoomed off. The cats arched their backs and circled us, hissing angrily.
They were going to attack us!

Then I remembered my Supersonic Screecher. I pulled it out of my pocket and let rip…

The cats fled, and I turned the Screecher off. The silence of the woods hung in my ears.

'Look to the skies.' The words from the letter rang in my head like an alarm bell.

An Adventure must be about to begin, I knew that much from the letter.

But who or what were the Partek?

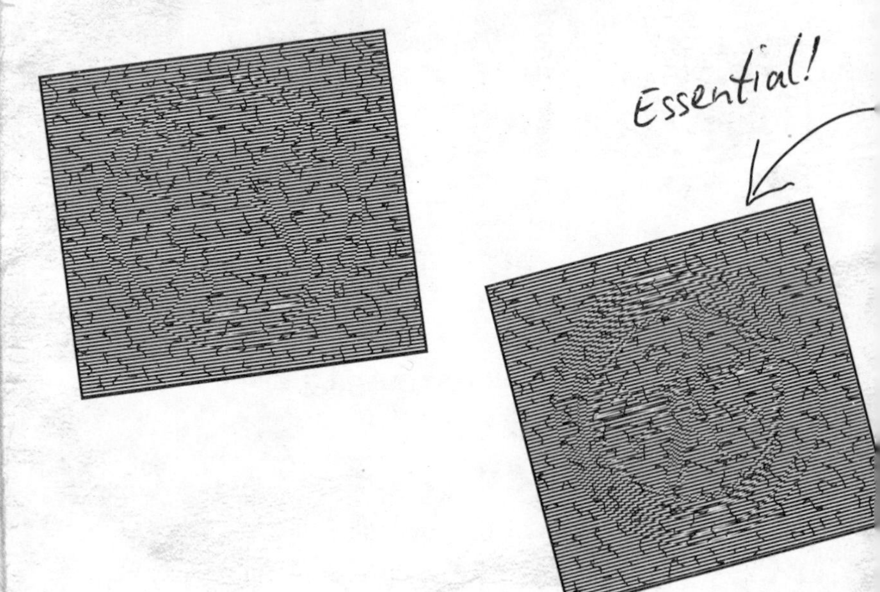

CHAPTER THREE
FACE AT THE WINDOW

I didn't get a chance to talk to Zoe about what we saw that night. We were both too busy trying to survive the school camping trip.

In the morning we cooked porridge on camping stoves and then we were sent orienteering. In case you're wondering, it's where you go off with a map and a compass and have to make your own way back. It was pouring with rain, and we ended up having to lug heavy backpacks. I couldn't wait till it was all over and we were packing up our tents and getting on the coach.

I read my grandpa's spy diary on the coach ride back. If I could find something in it about who was sending the letters, I could ask them to explain a few things – like who the Partek were.

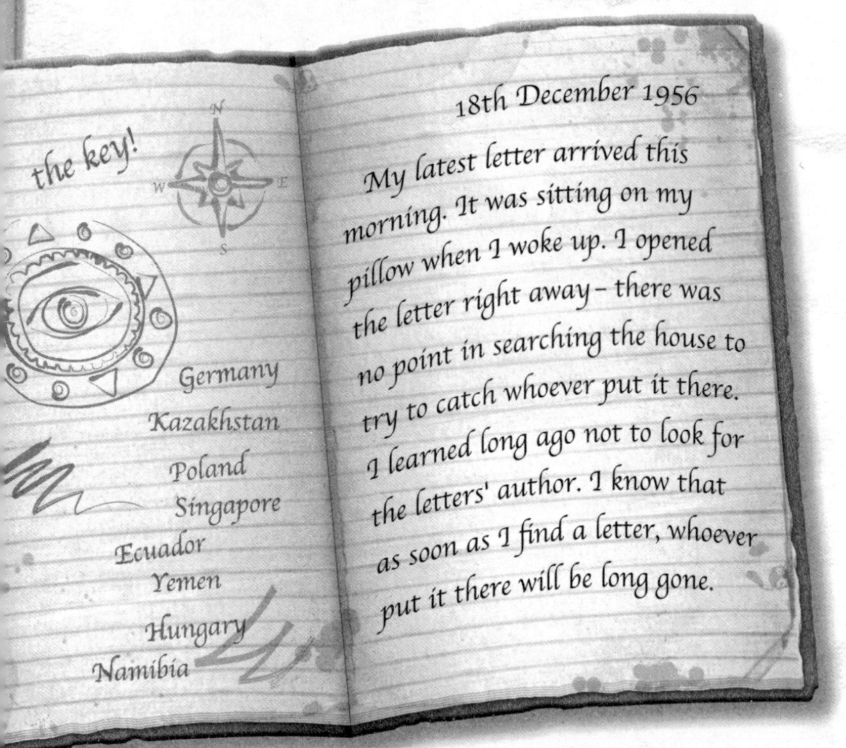

I flicked through some more diary entries. There was loads of stuff about a secret bunker, tips on how to spot a spy, and a list of countries Grandpa had entered with fake passports.

Grandpa had drawn a symbol on several pages. It was the same symbol as the one on an amulet I wore around my neck. It had been given to me in one of my previous letters, but I still didn't know what the symbol stood for.

The amulet works as a key when you press it against something that has the same symbol. I used it to open the box that had Grandpa's spy diary inside.

When the bus pulled into the school car park, I could see Stanley already waiting there to drive me home. Stanley is my grandpa's chauffeur. He also does loads of stuff around the house and generally helps Grandpa out. Stanley used to work in the White House for the President – pretty cool, huh?

I quickly said goodbye to Zoe and climbed into the car. Stanley drove me home in silence. That's another thing about Stanley – he hardly ever talks.

Eventually, the car pulled into the gates of Solvit Hall and drove down the mile-long driveway to the front door. I jumped out, slamming the car door behind me. Before I could even get my bag from the boot I heard Plato's manic yapping. (Plato's my grandpa's terrier. He's tiny, white and fluffy with very messy hair. He looks a lot like

Grandpa Monty!)

Anyway, Plato came rocketing towards me, his pink tongue hanging out of his mouth and his crazy snow-white fur bouncing up and down.

"How was Timbuktu?" My grandpa's voice came from inside the house.

"I wasn't in Timbuktu, Grandpa," I said, shutting the front door behind me. "I was on a school camping trip."

"Well, it would have been much more interesting if you'd gone to Timbuktu." Grandpa hobbled towards me on his cane and gave my hair a ruffle.

Grandpa Monty may be as loopy as a roller-coaster, but he's pretty cool really.

"If you could put young Henry's bag in his room, that would be marvellous," Grandpa said as Stanley started to climb the winding staircase with my heavy bag.

I raised my eyebrows. Henry is my dad's name, but Grandpa always calls me it by mistake. In fact, Grandpa Monty hardly ever remembers my actual name – he calls me all kinds of crazy things.

"Glass of milk?" Grandpa smiled at me.

"Yes, thank you," I said.

"We're having biscuits for dinner," Grandpa said as he headed into the kitchen. "I don't think we have any other food in the house."

Biscuits for dinner = fine by me!

Grandpa opened the fridge and poured two tall glasses of milk. He handed one to me and took a loud slurp from the other himself.

"I found a letter in a tree when I was camping," I said casually.

Grandpa was silent. He hated talking about

Adventurer stuff, especially letters.

"The letter said something about the Partek coming..."

Grandpa sat down and opened the newspaper, ignoring me completely.

"Me and Zoe were out in the woods, and there was this flying saucer in the sky, and it was beaming light on a group of cats, and then the cats tried to attack us..."

"How is Zoe?" Grandpa said suddenly. "When are you going to invite her over for dinner?"

"Don't try to change the subject, Grandpa. I don't believe for one second that you don't know anything about the Partek," I said angrily. "Didn't you come across them when you were an Adventurer?"

"Sometimes, Will," Grandpa said quietly as

he turned a page of his paper, "sometimes knowledge can't be taught. A wise man is wise because he searches the world for knowledge. If the world brought it to him, then he wouldn't be wise at all."

"What?" I raised my eyebrows.

"Kippers!" Grandpa shouted as he leaped up from his chair, grabbed his cane, and headed for the cupboard.

"Grandpa?"

"I have some old kippers that we can have for dinner. They were your father's favourite. He ate them every day when he was a boy."

"I'm not hungry," I snapped.

Annoyed, I headed for my room.

I was traipsing up the stairs when I saw an envelope with my name on it sitting on the top of the staircase.

HOW DID THE ASTRONAUT SERVE DRINKS?
IN SUNGLASSES.

EVIL IS COMING. THE PARTEK ARE COMING.
THERE IS A PLACE ABOVE THE EARTH. THIS PLACE
HOLDS THE SECRET TO WHAT IS GOING ON. YOU MUST GO
THERE AND SAVE THE WORLD. YOU MUST MAKE
A JOURNEY TO THIS CITY.
THE FIRST LETTER IS IN CRIB, BUT NOT IN CRIME.
THE SECOND LETTER IS A PERFECT SPHERE.
THE THIRD LETTER COMES AFTER R.
THE FOURTH LETTER IS ALSO THE NAME OF A DRINK.
THE FIFTH LETTER IS THE SAME AS THE SECOND.
THE SIXTH LETTER BEGINS NOVEMBER.

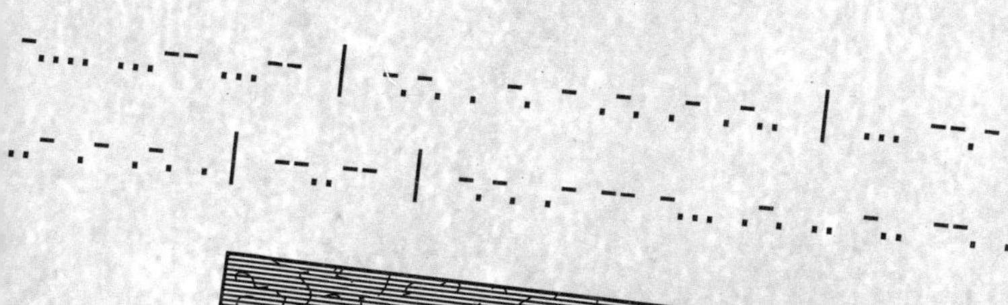

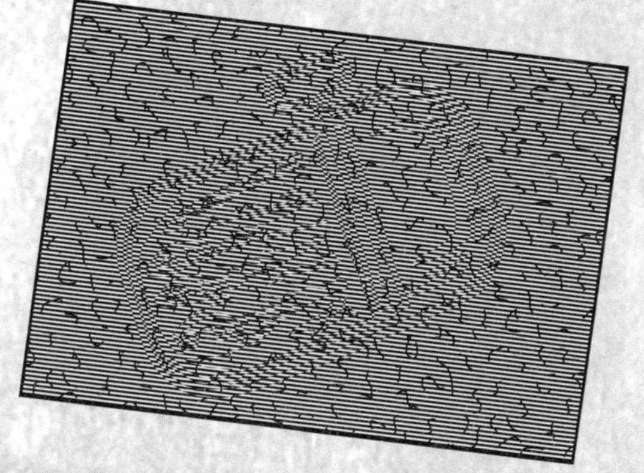

My heart was pounding as I began to add up the clues that I already had…

- **A place above the Earth = A place in space.**
- **Evil + the Partek = The Partek are evil.**
- **Space + Partek = The Partek are aliens.**

I was going into space to save the world from evil aliens – unbelievable!

I couldn't wait to get the Adventure underway. But first I had to do what the letter was telling me – I had to go on a journey.

I had to think for a while about the clues to the city name – but after a while I got it. The answer was Boston. I had to go to Boston! But I had no idea where in Boston I had to go.

Maybe the best thing would be to turn Morph into a computer and use the Internet to translate the Morse code at the bottom of the letter. So I ran to my bedroom, dug Morph out of my bag (it was still in the shape of the MP3 player I'd used during the camping trip). Flicking through Morph's computer chips, I found one called 'Laptop'. I activated it by pressing my thumb down on the X-ray pad and waited impatiently for Morph to morph into a laptop.

The tiny MP3 player began to shake and vibrate so quickly that all I could see was a blur of colours. The blur changed shape and grew larger, and the shaking slowed down, and suddenly Morph turned into a state-of-the-art laptop.

I logged onto the

Internet and typed 'Morse code translator' into the search engine. I clicked on the first option that came up – success! I carefully tapped the Morse code symbols into the decoder, and this is what it said...

633 Central Square, Cambridge

It was an address – and I bet every comic book I owned that it was where I needed to go. I knew that Cambridge was right across the river from Boston – and to get there from where I was, I would have to go to Boston first.

I was about to log off when I saw an instant message pop up on Morph's screen. It was from 'SingaporeSista' – Zoe.

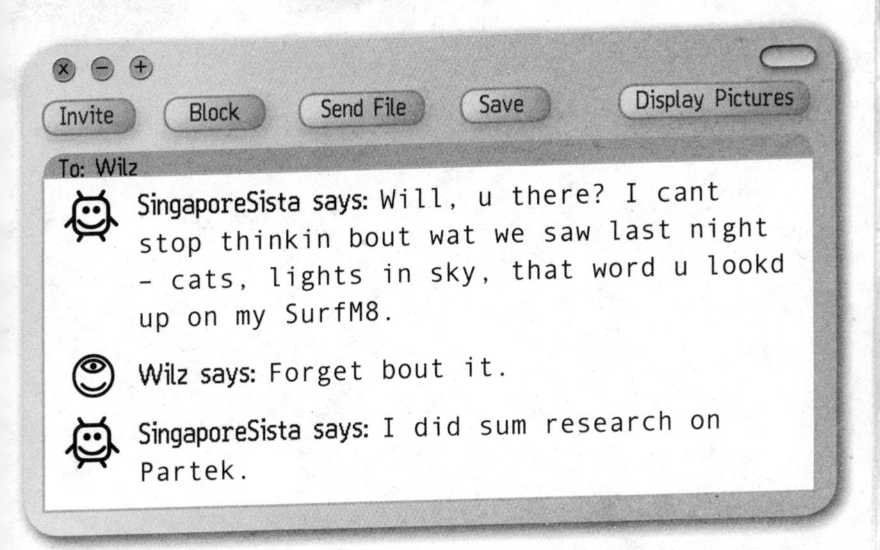

OK, now I was interested. I needed to know exactly what she knew.

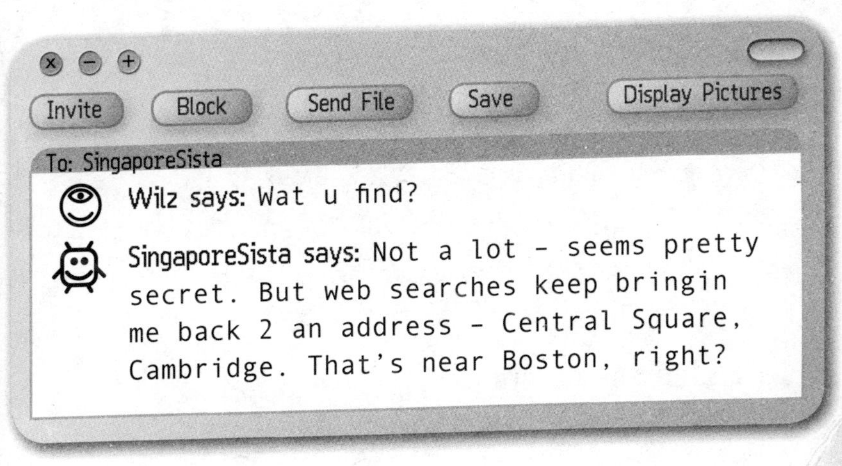

My heart jumped up and down as I reread the words on the computer screen. Central Square, Cambridge – that's where I had to go.

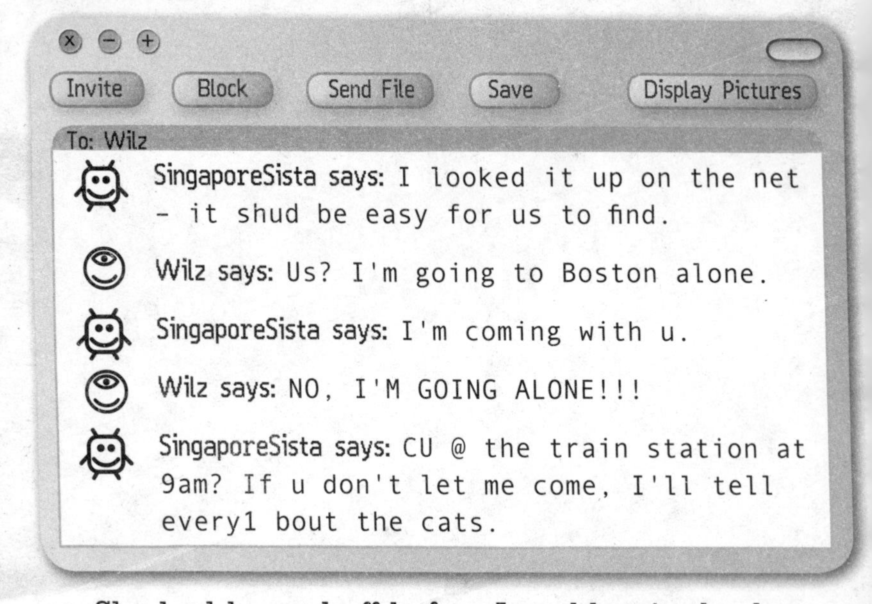

She had logged off before I could write back.

So that was that. I was going to Boston and Zoe was coming with me.

Turning the computer off, I sat on my bed to

read a comic book. But I kept hearing a funny noise at the window – it was horrible, as if someone was scratching a plate with a fork. Pulling back the curtain, I nearly keeled over and dropped dead with shock...

Staring back at me was the face of a cat. And not just any old cat – a giant cat, scratching its claws down the window. It hissed when it saw me. I stepped towards the window to get a better look, but just as I did the cat disappeared. I pressed my face against the window and saw what could only have been a hovering spacecraft blast off into the sky...

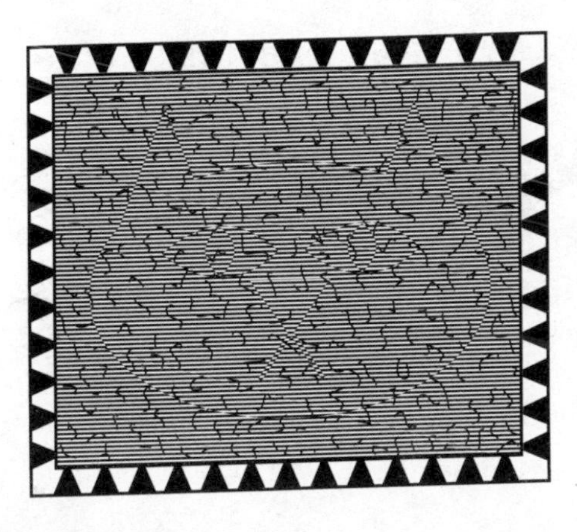

CHAPTER FOUR
THE BIG CITY

I'd only been to Boston three times in my whole life – once when Dad took me on a trip to the Museum of Natural History (they have a great bug collection: beetles, scorpions, cockroaches – everything!). Then once when we went to the theatre as a family, and then another time when I went shopping with Mum (boring). Boston is old, busy and bursting with history – I love it!

My alarm went off at 8:00 the next morning, but I was already awake and getting ready. I stuffed as many things as I could into my bag: my catapult, an omnilume (one of Dad's inventions – a stick that turns night to day), and Morph. That's the great thing about Morph. Once you've finished using it, it shrinks down to pocket-size in the exact form you were last using it.

I ran downstairs and into the kitchen to tell Grandpa I was going.

"Grandpa, Grandpa!" I yelled.

"No need to shout," Grandpa said calmly.

"I'm going to meet Zoe," I said.

"Shush! I'm trying to read," Grandpa spluttered through a mouthful of toast.

"OK, bye!" I called as I ran out of the kitchen. Phew, I didn't even have to tell him where exactly I was going.

I slung my bag over my shoulder and got into the car with Stanley.

I swear I noticed more cats than usual out on the street as we drove. Every one of them looked dangerous. Sounds weird, but believe me, if you'd seen them you'd have been freaked out too. They were walking around with their backs arched and their claws digging into the ground.

Zoe was waiting outside the train station when Stanley dropped me off. Zoe had already bought the tickets and we only had to wait for a few minutes before the train arrived.

"Um, Will?" Zoe said as we sat down.

"Yeah?"

"I thought you might want this..." she opened her bag and pulled out a SurfM8 50 – an older version of the SurfM8 60, but still pretty cool.

"You're giving me your old SurfM8?" I asked, astonished.

"My dad always sends me the newest gadgets from Singapore, and I don't use it any more. I thought you could use it to IM me," she said.

"WOW! Thanks, Zoe!" I beamed as I took the SurfM8 from her. It was black with a silver rim around the edges. The keypad and screen looked brand new – like they hadn't even been used.

We spent the rest of the ride talking about SurfM8s, spaceships (Zoe didn't believe in aliens) and cats. It turns out that Zoe's always thought cats were evil. Neither of us could figure out what cats had to do with aliens, though.

We got to Boston and headed for the underground. Zoe had downloaded an underground map from the Internet, which showed us which line we needed. The train was packed all the way to Central Square.

Outside the station, we walked around until we found number 633.

Everywhere we looked there were more cats than people – cats walking along the street, cats running down the road, even a black cat in the back of a taxi! What was going on?

At last we found number 633. There was a plaque on the wall that said 'National Scientific Academy'.

"What are we going to say when we get in?" Zoe asked.

"Let me do the talking," I told her.

I walked straight up to the door and pressed the buzzer.

"Hello," said a voice on the intercom.

"Hi," I said back. "I'm here to see my dad. Can you let me in, please?"

"Who's your father?" asked the voice.

I put my hands across my mouth so my voice was muffled. "Abhhher Soeerr," I mumbled into the intercom.

"Hang on," said the voice on the intercom. "I'll come and let you in."

Success!

The heavy door swung open and a sweaty security guard stood in front of us.

"Thanks!" I said as I walked past him and into the building. Zoe skipped in behind me. "I'm here to see my dad," I said as I looked around and saw a sign that said 'Experimental Astrophysics' pointing down a narrow staircase.

"He works down there," I said.

"Wait there," ordered the security guard.

He disappeared into his office and I heard him pick up a phone and start tapping numbers into it.

"Quick!" I whispered to Zoe, bolting towards the staircase as fast as a cheetah being rocketed along by turbo farts. Zoe followed me.

At the bottom of the staircase there was a long corridor. The first door on the left was slightly open, so I ducked in, quickly followed by Zoe.

We were in some kind of a large storeroom with

rows and rows of shelves stacked full of jars.

"What is this place?" asked Zoe.

I walked up to one of the jars to get a better look. Inside was what looked like a hand, but it was covered with scales. The hand had seven fingers, and instead of nails it had metal-looking claws at the end of each finger.

"Will, what is this stuff? It's freaking me out."

"Chill, Zoe," I said quietly as I studied the jars.

On a shelf way above my head, I saw an envelope with my name on it between two of the jars. I looked around for a stool, or something I could stand on to reach it – there was nothing.

Awesome!

"What's wrong? What are you looking for?" Zoe asked nervously.

"Nothing," I snapped. I didn't want her to know about the letter, but I needed to get it down.

"Um, can you stick your head out of the door," I said to her, "to make sure no one followed us?"

"No way!" she said. "You got us in here, you go and check. And anyway, there's something up there between those jars."

"It's probably nothing," I said calmly, trying to distract her.

"It has your name on it!" she exclaimed. "Let's get it down fast, before someone finds us."

I went over and reluctantly clasped my hands together before putting them out for Zoe to climb into. As I lifted her up, she reached for the top shelf and grabbed my letter. I lowered her down and snatched the envelope out of her hands before ripping it open.

WHAT ILLNESS DID EVERYONE ON THE ENTERPRISE CATCH?

CHICKEN SPOCKS!

CONGRATULATIONS ON GETTING HERE.

THE DANGEROUS PART IS JUST BEGINNING.

-.. --- --- .-. | -... . ... -. -.. |

-.-. .- -... .. -. . -

Zoe dug her SurfM8 out of her bag and started tapping in the code to translate it.

Suddenly we could hear the sound of heavy footsteps on a creaking staircase, and then voices outside. The security guard was coming after us – and he wasn't alone.

"HIDE!" I warned Zoe.

"Will, the code in the letter..." Zoe said,

studying the screen of her SurfM8. "It says something about a door..."

The voices and footsteps stopped outside the room. The doorknob started to rattle.

"Behind the cabinet!" Zoe whispered quickly. "The code says there's a door behind the cabinet."

Just as the security guard closed in on us, we shot towards a large filing cabinet at the back of the room. I took my catapult out of my bag and pulled a large stone from my pocket.

Raising the catapult, I aimed at a unit of shelves on the other side of the room. I pulled back the elastic and let it snap free. The stone flew through the air and smashed two jars to smithereens.

"Over there!" The security guards ran towards the smashed glass. Excellent! I'd sent them in the wrong direction.

Zoe and I pulled the cabinet away from the wall.
KLK!
Zoe was right – there was a door! It opened to reveal a tunnel.
It was pitch black inside the tunnel. Good thing I remembered to bring an omnilume!
The ceiling was low – at some points we had to crawl. We passed dozens of tiny doors.
TOP
ECRET
DANGE

Finally, we came to a door that said...
TOP SECRET DARE CHAMBER
I turned the handle, my heart pounding. The door creaked open.
TOP SECRET DARE CHAMBER
There was a single table in the middle of the room. On the table was a box.
The symbol on top of the box matched my amulet.

"Looks like we're going to need a key to open it," said Zoe.

"No problem," I mumbled, pulling the amulet out from under my T-shirt.

Zoe looked at me, stunned. I knew I'd have a lot of explaining to do, but right then I didn't care.

I held the amulet towards the box. It didn't surprise me when it clicked open. This time there were no diaries inside the box, just one small scrap of paper.

I lifted it up and read it out loud:

SECRET COORDINATES OF THE DARE SATELLITE:
49 AU, 25.5°

Getting out of the Top Secret DARE Chamber was much easier than getting in. There was a door on the other side of the room that led to a lift, and inside the lift was a button that said 'Street'. I pushed the button and the lift whizzed up and opened to the outside.

"We need to get away from here – fast," I said and started running down the street towards the underground station. Zoe ran behind me.

My head was spinning with a billion questions. What was the DARE Satellite?

Why did the symbol on the amulet keep popping up everywhere? And did the Partek have anything to do with DARE?

"I think we should head for home," Zoe said as

we stepped onto the train. "I know the piece of paper in the box said something about a satellite. But we don't exactly have a way of blasting into outer space, do we?"

I nodded silently. She was right about one thing – it was time to go home. But she was wrong about not having a way to blast into outer space. I knew exactly how I could get there: Morph.

We were both pretty subdued as we arrived at North Station and made our way to the train that would take us back.

Zoe bombarded me with words as soon as we were sitting in an empty car. "What...amulet... letter...secret door...satellite?"

"Calm down," I told her. "You sound like a demented chipmunk when you talk that fast."

"You owe me the truth." Her voice trembled.

Before I could think of something clever to say,

the doors flung open and three girls came in. They were older than us, stank of flowery perfume, and were carrying a billion shopping bags. There was no way I was saying anything with those girls around, so Zoe and I didn't speak for the rest of the journey.

It was half-past six by the time we got off the train. I hadn't eaten much all day and I was starving.

"I'm going to call my mum and let her know I'm going to your house," Zoe announced.

"I don't remember inviting you...."

But Zoe was already punching in the numbers.

We walked all the way back to my house to find Grandpa and Plato waiting for us at the front door.

"Hungry, Oliver?" Grandpa asked me. "How about some kippers?"

Yuck.

"My name's Will, Grandpa," I reminded him. "And I don't really like kippers. Can I just have biscuits for dinner?"

"How about a biscuit-and-kipper pie?"

I took a sideways glance at Zoe and watched as Grandpa opened a can and put some smelly kippers on a plate. I couldn't tell if he was joking or not.

Grandpa hobbled to the biscuit tin and pulled out a handful of soggy chocolate biscuits. I watched as he started to crumble them over the kippers. He wasn't joking at all – he was actually making a biscuit-and-kipper pie. Double yuck!

"Uh, Grandpa," I laughed, "if it's OK with you, I think I'll just have the biscuits."

"Up to you," Grandpa said as he started to spoon the biscuit-and-kipper pie into his mouth.

Zoe sat at the kitchen table and looked at me

and Grandpa as if she was having dinner at the zoo.

After eating we headed upstairs.

Once we were in my room, Zoe folded her arms and looked at me seriously. "Will, what is going on?"

"Nothing!" I turned on the TV and started flicking through the channels, trying to distract her.

"If you don't tell me, I'll ask your grandpa, my mum, Mrs Simmons, and every other grown-up I know."

I flicked the TV to a show about cats.

Zoe started to storm out of the room.

"Wait!" I shouted at her. "Promise you won't tell?"

"Cross my heart."

"OK..."

I keep every letter I've ever been sent in a box under my bed. I pulled out the box and nervously handed it to Zoe. She started to read my letters, one by one.

I felt weird about her reading them, so I looked at the TV instead. But every channel had nothing but news! BORING!! Then I couldn't help but hear what one reporter was saying... "Reports of cats attacking their owners have now reached the thousands."

The same news story was being reported on every single channel – it was serious. Since the appearance of lights in the sky, it seemed that cats all over the world had been going AWOL.

"Zoe..." I said, pointing to the TV. "The cats must be connected to the lights in the..."

"There's a letter here that hasn't been opened," Zoe said, holding up an envelope with my name on it.

I tore the envelope open and pulled out the letter inside.

```
--. --- | - --- | - .... . | -.. .- .-. . | ... .-
- . .-.. .-.. .. - . | .-.-.- | ... - --- .--. | - ....
. | .--. .- .-. - . -.- | .-.-.- | --. --- | .- .-..
--- -. . | .-.-.- |
```

Morse code again.

Before I could do anything, Zoe had her SurfM8 in her hand and was typing furiously. She held up the screen to me so I could see what the Morse code meant.

Go to the DARE Satellite. Stop the Partek.
Go alone.

So the Partek and the DARE Satellite were definitely connected.

"They must be talking about aliens," Zoe said.

"And the DARE Satellite is where I have to go," I said quietly. It was all starting to make sense.

"But why you, Will?" Zoe asked. "You're only ten, how can you help?" She began to laugh. "And anyway, how are you going to get into space?"

"Zoe!" I heard Grandpa call from downstairs. "Your mother is here to take you home."

"We'll talk about this at school tomorrow," she said seriously.

"If I'm not there, send a search party," I joked. She didn't laugh.

Without another word, Zoe turned and bolted out of the room.

I was quiet for a while as I sat on my bed, thinking about what I had to do. A shiver of excitement ran through me. This was my first official Adventure – I had to go into outer space to save the world from aliens. It doesn't get much more incredible than that!

Dad had taught me the basics of space travel: don't go outside the spaceship without a space suit, strap yourself in until you leave Earth's atmosphere, etc. But anything I didn't know, I was going to have to make up as I went along.

I packed my bag, taking an omnilume, invisibility paint, the SurfM8 50, Dad's stun gun, my compass that always points home, the Supersonic Screecher and Grandpa's diary.

I found Morph's 'Spaceship' memory chip and headed for the back garden. I activated Morph and watched as it turned into a fully operational, super-turbo spaceship. (In case you're wondering why I haven't just used Morph as a time machine to rescue Mum and Dad, the answer's simple – Morph's time machine program is broken.)

I stepped inside the spaceship and entered the coordinates of the DARE Satellite into the control panel. The spaceship flashed and flickered into life. Now there was only one thing left to do...

I pressed the button marked 'TAKE OFF'.

It took thirty minutes to soar through the Earth's atmosphere. I used the time to translate the Morse code in Grandpa's diary entries. The SurfM8 even worked in space!

25th July 1957

The Department of Astronomical Research and Experimentation is building a top-secret satellite. The satellite will be used to monitor the Partek.

It will be called the DARE Satellite, after the department.

Nothing as ambitious as sending humans into space has ever been attempted before. It must be kept a secret from the general public for their own good.

As an Adventurer, I will do everything within my power to protect the Earth. I will make certain that every Adventurer who lives after me does too.

So what did the Partek look like? I couldn't believe I was about to see a real live alien. I was so excited, I felt like I'd swallowed a yo-yo!

As soon as Morph blasted out of Earth's atmosphere, I unbuckled my seat belt and started to float. I could do somersaults, jumping jacks and the Running Man without touching the floor.

When I got over the excitement of floating, I took a look out of Morph's spaceship window.

We were passing Mars, which looked like red rocky mountains. We curved past Jupiter, weaving

WILL'S FACT FILE

Dear Adventurer,

You probably already know that our planet is part of a solar system of eight planets. You also probably know that we travel around one star – the Sun.

What you probably *don't* know is the cool stuff inside this Fact File. Check out the facts and timeline and expand your space knowledge. There are a few extra notes from me, in case you need them, and some space mysteries for you to think about...

Space Travel

1942
Germany launch the V2 rocket, which was the first object to reach 100 km from the Earth's surface.

1947
The first animals were blasted into space. Scientists chose fruit flies to be the lucky creatures.

1957
Russia launched the first satellite into space: Sputnik 1. 'Sputnik' means 'satellite' in Russian.

1961
Russian Cosmonaut Yuri Gagarin became the first man in space. His spacecraft completed one orbit of Earth before crash-landing back down.

1963
Valentina Tereshkova became the first woman to blast into space.

1965
Another Russian Cosmonaut, Aleksei Leonov, was the first person to spacewalk.

1969
On 20th July, Apollo 11 touched down on the Moon and Neil Armstrong was the first person to moonwalk!

1971
Russia launched the first space station, Salyut 1.

1971
First non-manned spacecraft landed on Mars.

1975
Non-manned spacecraft completed the first orbit around Venus.

1989
Voyager 2 flies by Neptune – that's a long way from Earth!

2001
An American man called Dennis Tito was the first space tourist.

2004
US President George Bush announced that NASA would resume missions to the Moon by 2020, and work on a permanent Moon-base would begin.

2005
First non-manned spacecraft landed on Titan, which is one of Saturn's moons.

THE FUTURE!
NASA is planning a manned mission to Mars. This won't happen for a few more years yet, so one of the astronauts on board could b...

The International Space Station

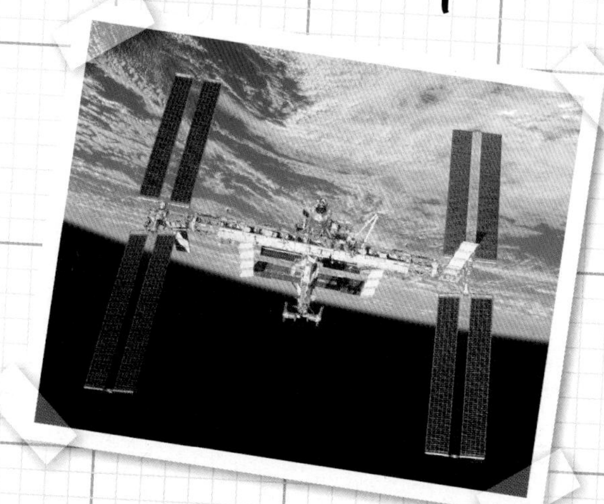

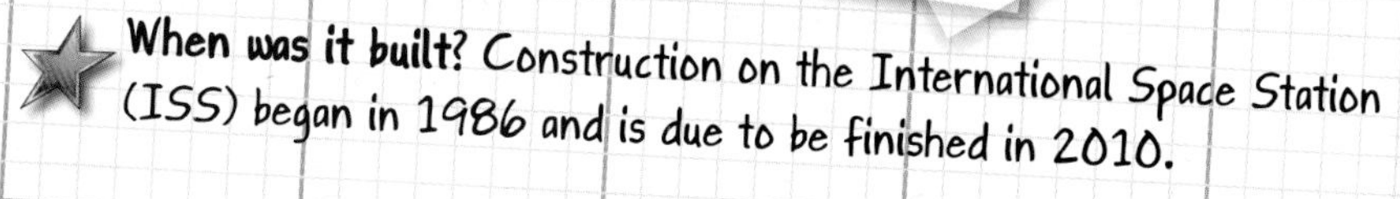

When was it built? Construction on the International Space Station (ISS) began in 1986 and is due to be finished in 2010.

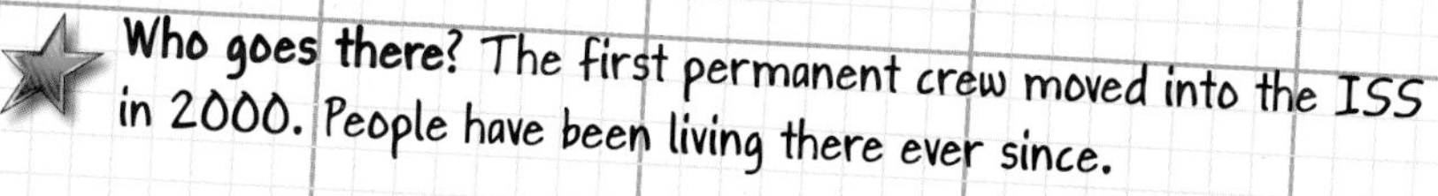

Who goes there? The first permanent crew moved into the ISS in 2000. People have been living there ever since.

Where is it? The ISS orbits between 320 to 350 km above the Earth's surface.

Why is it there? It provides a base in space from which astronauts can conduct their research and exploration.

What's on it? Onboard the ISS there are areas for astronauts to sleep, exercise and perform experiments.

What kind of experiments? Experiments in physics, biology, astronomy, meteorology and zero gravity. Cool!

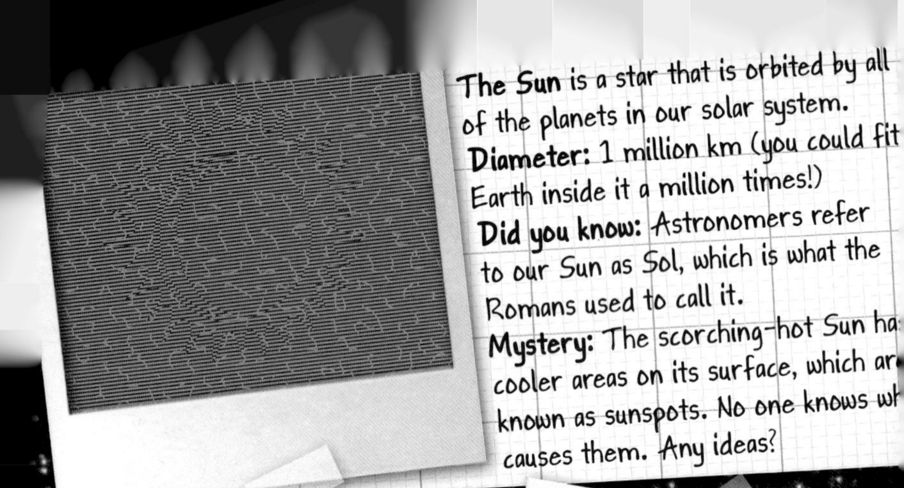

The Sun is a star that is orbited by all of the planets in our solar system.
Diameter: 1 million km (you could fit Earth inside it a million times!)
Did you know: Astronomers refer to our Sun as Sol, which is what the Romans used to call it.
Mystery: The scorching-hot Sun ha[s] cooler areas on its surface, which ar[e] known as sunspots. No one knows wh[at] causes them. Any ideas?

A comet is made of rock, ice and dust and has a tail called a 'coma'.
Diameter: 100 m to 40 km across
Time to orbit the Sun: Varies
Did you know: 'Comet' comes from the Greek 'kome', meaning 'hair of the head' because Aristotle described comets as 'stars with hair'.
Mystery: A comet's tail is only visible when it's near the Sun. Why do you think this is?

A black hole forms when pressure forces a dying star to become smaller and smaller, unti[l] it is smaller than an atom.
Did you know: Black holes are like vacuum cleaners – they suck up debris from outer space. They us[e] the power of gravity to pull things towards them.
Mystery: Where does debris g[o] when it's inside a black hole?

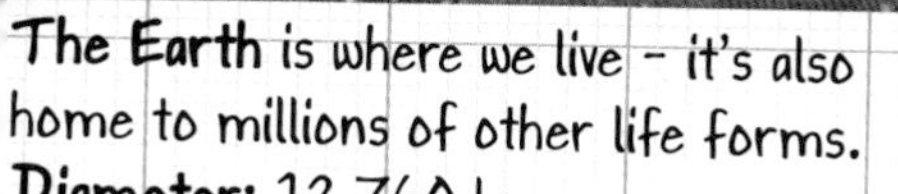

The Earth is where we live – it's also home to millions of other life forms.
Diameter: 12,760 km
Time to orbit the Sun: 1 year
Did you know: 71% of the Earth's surface is covered by water.
Mystery: As far as we know, Earth is the only planet in our solar system that can support life. Could there be a way to change the atmosphere on other planets so that we could live there?

The Moon is Earth's natural satellite. It received its first human footprint in 1969 and because there is no wind on the Moon, it will be there for a million years!
Diameter: 3,474 km
Time to orbit Earth: 27.3 days
Did you know: The Moon's gravitational pull causes most of Earth's tides.
Mystery: There is no 'dark side' of the Moon. So why do we always seem to see the same face of the Moon?

Jupiter is a giant planet that has at least 63 moons.
Diameter: 143,800 km
Time to orbit the Sun: 11.86 years
Did you know: The large red spot on Jupiter's surface is actually a giant storm that has been raging for at least 300 years.
Mystery: How is it possible for a storm to last 300 years?

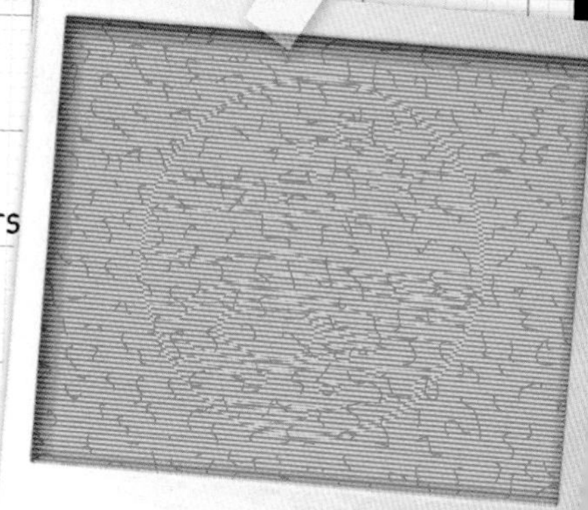

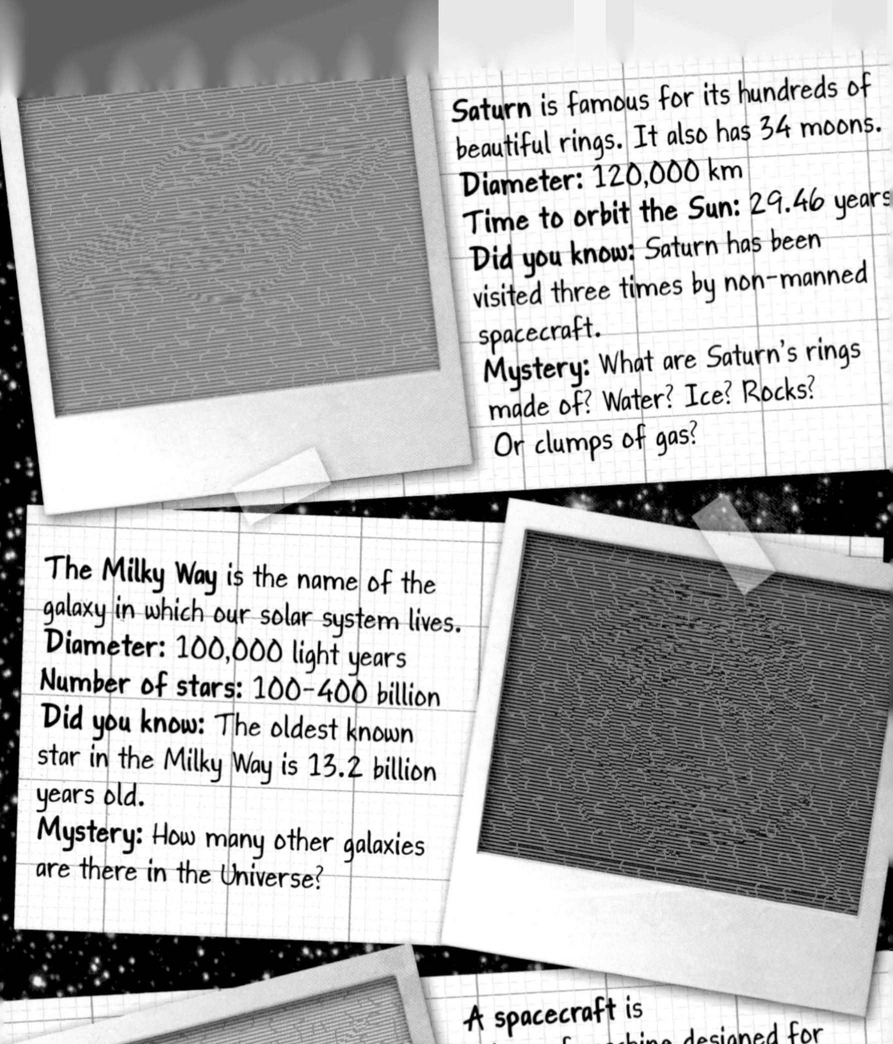

Saturn is famous for its hundreds of beautiful rings. It also has 34 moons.
Diameter: 120,000 km
Time to orbit the Sun: 29.46 years
Did you know: Saturn has been visited three times by non-manned spacecraft.
Mystery: What are Saturn's rings made of? Water? Ice? Rocks? Or clumps of gas?

The Milky Way is the name of the galaxy in which our solar system lives.
Diameter: 100,000 light years
Number of stars: 100–400 billion
Did you know: The oldest known star in the Milky Way is 13.2 billion years old.
Mystery: How many other galaxies are there in the Universe?

A spacecraft is a type of machine designed for travelling in space.
Did you know: The space shuttle was the first type of spacecraft to be used more than once. Some shuttles can complete over 100 space missions.
Mystery: If you could design your own ultimate spacecraft, what would it look like?

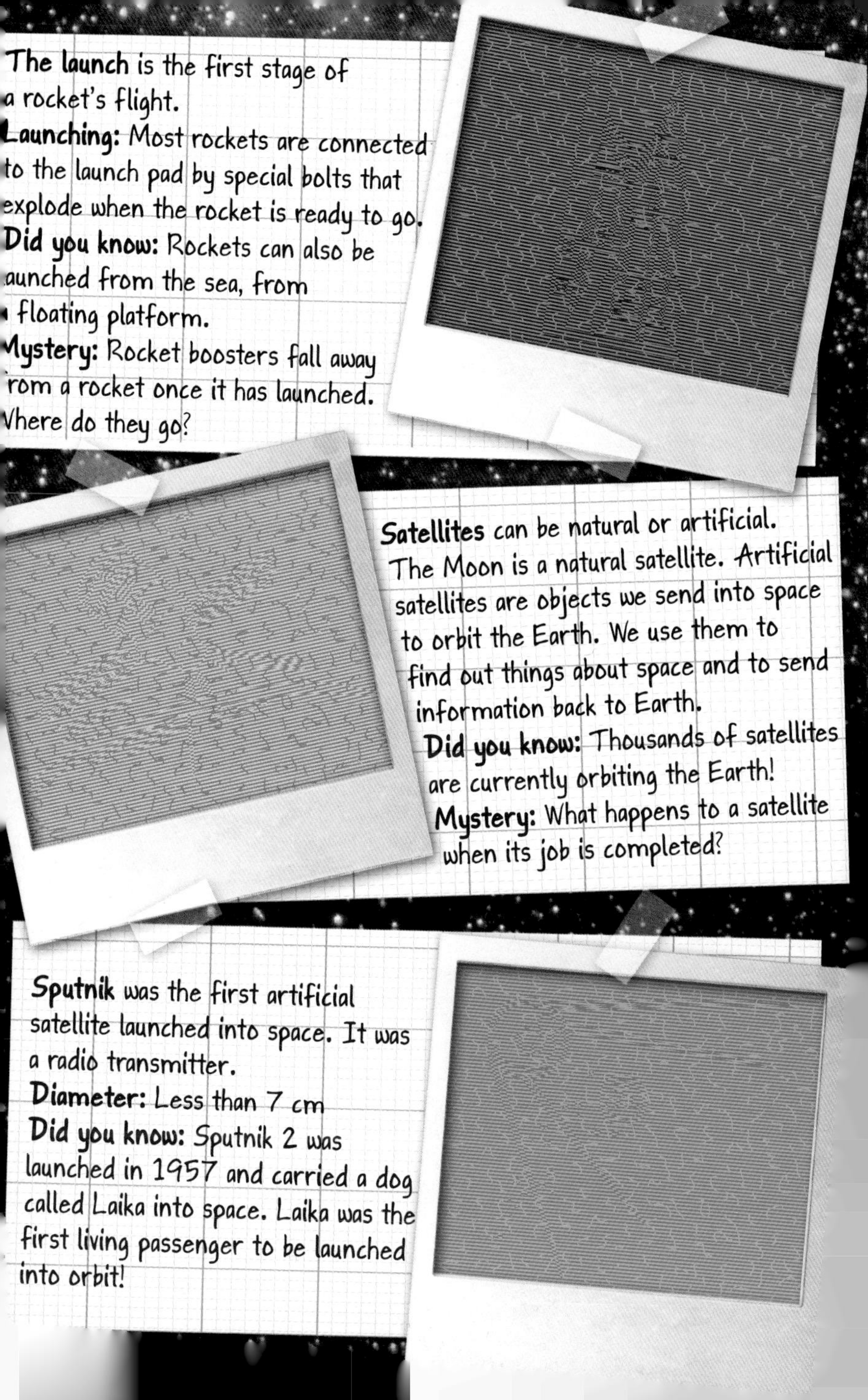

The launch is the first stage of a rocket's flight.
Launching: Most rockets are connected to the launch pad by special bolts that explode when the rocket is ready to go.
Did you know: Rockets can also be launched from the sea, from a floating platform.
Mystery: Rocket boosters fall away from a rocket once it has launched. Where do they go?

Satellites can be natural or artificial. The Moon is a natural satellite. Artificial satellites are objects we send into space to orbit the Earth. We use them to find out things about space and to send information back to Earth.
Did you know: Thousands of satellites are currently orbiting the Earth!
Mystery: What happens to a satellite when its job is completed?

Sputnik was the first artificial satellite launched into space. It was a radio transmitter.
Diameter: Less than 7 cm
Did you know: Sputnik 2 was launched in 1957 and carried a dog called Laika into space. Laika was the first living passenger to be launched into orbit!

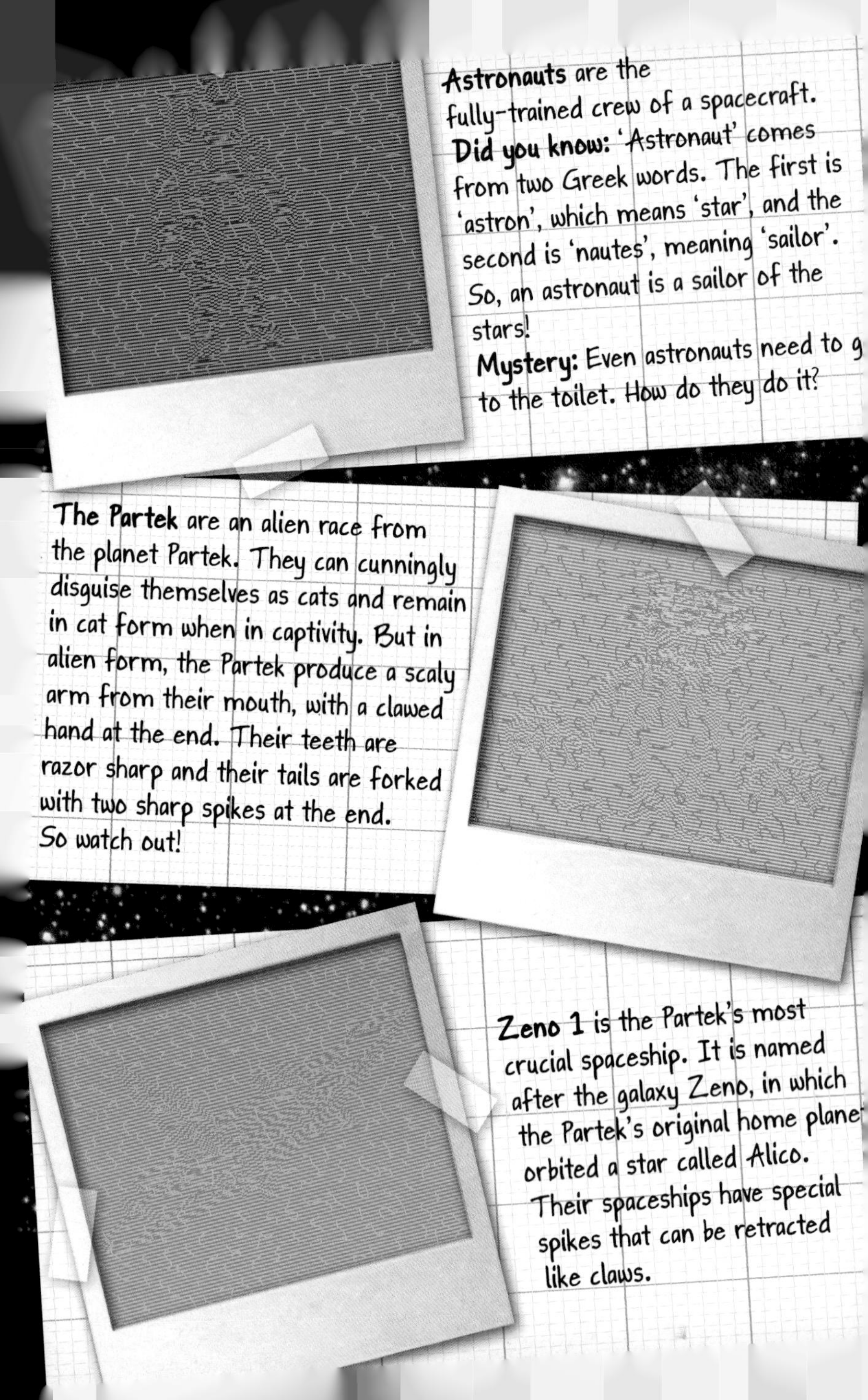

Astronauts are the fully-trained crew of a spacecraft.

Did you know: 'Astronaut' comes from two Greek words. The first is 'astron', which means 'star', and the second is 'nautes', meaning 'sailor'. So, an astronaut is a sailor of the stars!

Mystery: Even astronauts need to g to the toilet. How do they do it?

The Partek are an alien race from the planet Partek. They can cunningly disguise themselves as cats and remain in cat form when in captivity. But in alien form, the Partek produce a scaly arm from their mouth, with a clawed hand at the end. Their teeth are razor sharp and their tails are forked with two sharp spikes at the end. So watch out!

Zeno 1 is the Partek's most crucial spaceship. It is named after the galaxy Zeno, in which the Partek's original home plane orbited a star called Alico. Their spaceships have special spikes that can be retracted like claws.

in and out of its colourful rings before shooting past Saturn, which was huge and yellow and had lots of moons.

Then Morph started making a beeping noise. I pulled my way to the control deck, panicking. But everything was OK. The spaceship's GPS system was just homing in on the DARE Satellite. We were getting closer.

Suddenly I felt as if I had grasshoppers partying in my stomach. I was so nervous. What was waiting for me on the satellite? How would I defeat the Partek? And maybe, just maybe, space travel could be my special Adventurer skill?

The journey had only taken me a couple of hours, but it felt like no time at all. I'm lucky that Morph can travel almost at the speed of light – otherwise it would have taken me a lifetime to get that far away from Earth.

The beeps on Morph's GPS monitor got faster and louder, and I looked out of the window to see a huge silver disc-shaped space station.

There was a button on Morph's spaceship control panel that said 'Invisibility Panels'. I didn't know how safe the satellite would be, and the last thing I wanted was for the Partek to see me flying towards them, so I pressed the button.

I took hold of the steering wheel and gently steered Morph towards the satellite, trying to keep my cool.

Morph picked up speed and started to veer to the right. I tried to steer the spaceship in a straight line, but something else was controlling Morph now, something inside the satellite.

Up close, the satellite looked like something out of Star Wars – like a city in a block of metal, floating around in space.

Then I had a brainstorm.

"Invisibility paint!" I shouted, as I dived for my backpack – that was my only chance of sneaking into the satellite undetected. I dunked my fingers into the tub and started painting myself from head to toe – being careful not to miss any bits. The paint dried quickly into sticky goo.

Then I looked ahead. Something on the satellite door caught my eye – a large symbol that I instantly recognized as the one on the amulet around my neck.

The inner satellite doors opened wide and Morph glided in.

I was blinded by a bright white light. When my eyes adjusted to the harsh glow, I could see people in white lab coats standing outside Morph.

They were waving their arms around in confusion and talking to one another. I'd turned Morph's invisibility panels on and no one could see the spaceship in front of them. But they must have known that there was something there, because the satellite doors had opened to let Morph in.

Morph's door swooshed open and I jumped out

Needed sunglasses!

onto a hard white floor. I could see more people, a lot of desks with computers, and a large door with an 'Entrance' sign on it. Everything was stark white.

Before anyone had a chance to come near Morph, I deactivated it to shrink back down into a pocket-sized spaceship and put it in my invisible bag.

Convinced that no one had seen me, I started to tiptoe towards the door. When I got there, I walked straight through it.

There was a long white corridor in front of me, which I ran down as quietly as I could.

My foot slipped on something, and I almost fell over. Looking down, I saw an envelope with my name on it. I read the letter quickly.

HOW DID THE ASTRONAUT SERVE DINNER IN OUTER SPACE?

ON FLYING SAUCERS.

THERE ISN'T MUCH TIME. YOU'RE ON THE DARE SATELLITE. THE PEOPLE YOU SEE ARE ALL SCIENTISTS. YOU NEED TO HEAD FOR THE FLOOR NAMED AFTER A PHILOSOPHER WHOSE NAME BEGINS WITH 'H' AND RHYMES WITH FUME.

WHEN YOU GET THERE, LOOK FOR THE ROOM THAT'S THE SQUARE ROOT OF 9.

.- | ..-. .. .. | -... . --. .. -. -. .. -. --. |
.-- .. - .... | -.- | --..-- | -... | .-.. . - - .
.-. ...

I knew what the square root of nine was – three. So I had to go to room number three on the floor named after a philosopher beginning with 'H' and rhyming with fume.

I heard footsteps in the distance so I shoved the letter into my pocket. It became invisible like the rest of me.

A man and woman in white coats were coming towards me. I pressed myself against the wall and listened as they walked past.

"Unless we know how the Partek are communicating with them," said the man, "I don't see what we can do."

"I know," the woman replied. "If we don't do something, Earth will be destroyed..."

The two scientists walked away and I quickly took out my SurfM8. I turned it on and quickly tapped in 'Philosophers H'. Loads of names came up: Hick, Hegel, Hippias, Hume. That had to be it!

I was just about to log on to the site that translates Morse code when an IM from Zoe popped up on the screen.

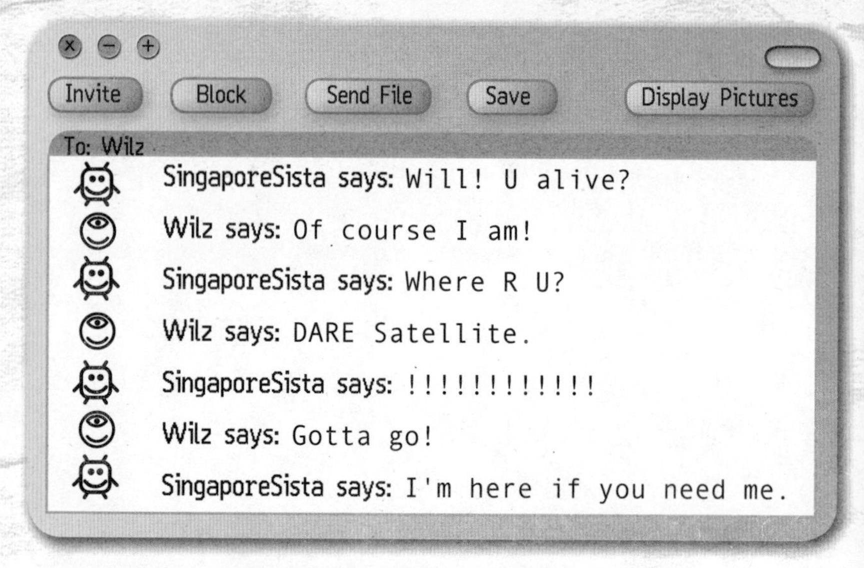

I didn't waste any more time. I'd have to translate the Morse code in my letter later. I ran through the corridor and eventually came to a large room with doors and staircases in every direction. There was a sign pointing to a flight of stairs that said 'Hume Deck', and I ran up. Soon I was in another corridor with numbered rooms. I made my way to number three.

I pulled my amulet out from under my T-shirt and pressed it against the symbol on the lock. The

Brrrr!

door clicked open, and I snuck into room three.

There were no people in the room. All I could see were hundreds of cabinets with frosted glass. I stepped closer to one of them to get a better look, peering through the glass. Inside was a small cat – it looked like it had been frozen stiff. The glass cabinets weren't cabinets at all – they were freezers!

I looked in a few of the other freezers, and sure enough, they all had cats frozen in them too. Without thinking, I pressed my amulet against the nearest lock and the freezer door sprang open.

The cat inside the freezer began to tremble. As the icicles around it began to melt, I could see that it was a ginger cat with huge black eyes and long whiskers.

The cat let out a pleased purr and jumped out of the freezer, landing at my feet.

As I bent down to pet him, the cat arched its back and hissed viciously. Then it got bigger...
I darted backwards. The cat beast shot its claws at me.
What are you?
Parrr-tek!

We have a code red!
How did it get out?
One of the professors tried to throw a net over the cat monster.
Heeelp!
I pulled out my dad's stun gun and blasted the cat with a bolt of blue electricity. It froze and began to shrink back down to normal pet size.

A man with a badge saying 'Professor Andrews' gazed in my direction. "What the…" he said.

I'd given myself away.

Quickly Professor Andrews put the small cat back into its cage and locked the door. Then he walked to the wall and turned off the alarm.

Suddenly everything was quiet.

"Henry Solvit?" a woman said quietly. Her badge said Dr Burden.

Henry Solvit? That was my dad's name! How did she know my dad? I was about to run from the room when I felt something wet rain down on me. Some kind of sprinkler system had been activated.

I looked down and saw the invisibility paint slide off my body into a glistening puddle on the floor.

The two scientists gazed at me in horror.

It was a while before they spoke.

Uh-oh!

"But... but..." stuttered Dr Burden, "you're a child."

I didn't know what to say, so I didn't say anything at all. I quietly put the stun gun back into my backpack and stood there until one of them spoke again.

"Who are you?" Professor Andrews asked me.

"I'm Will Solvit," I told him. "I'm Henry's son."

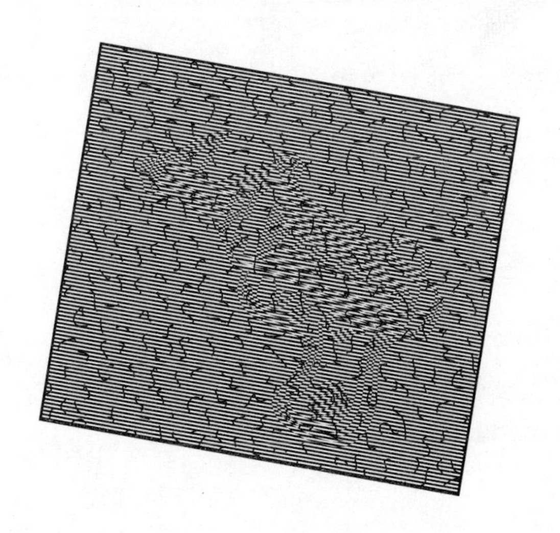

Professor Andrews and Dr Burden took me to a small room with nothing in it besides a chair.

"Hey, that's mine!" I shouted as they snatched the backpack out of my hands and started pulling out my tools.

"A radioactive stun gun, an omnilume, a handheld Internet device, a toy spaceship and a diary." Professor Andrews looked at me and squinted his eyes, "You've stolen these from Henry. How did you get here?"

"I haven't stolen anything," I said. "I'm here to help you. Aliens are going to attack Earth, and as much fun as it is talking to you," I said sarcastically, "you need to tell me how to stop them!"

Professor Andrews sighed and Dr Burden grunted in disapproval.

"What you just saw," Professor Andrews said slowly, "was a member of the Partek. The Partek can disguise themselves as cats, or be forced to remain in cat form when held in captivity. But when a Partek is free, it looks like the beast you saw a minute ago."

"And are the Partek planning to invade Earth?" I asked.

"Let me explain..." Professor Andrews continued. "Planet Partek once orbited a star called Alico in the Zeno galaxy. It was a beautiful and peaceful planet. For millions of years, the Partek race evolved and prospered."

"But the Partek are not a peaceful race," Dr Burden joined in. "They fought many wars and eventually destroyed their planet. The only way the Partek could survive was to build spaceships, blast into the skies, and discover a new world to inhabit. They destroyed every planet they found."

Professor Andrews took over. "For as long as man has looked at the stars, the Partek have been waiting for a time when they could invade Earth and claim it as their own. They'll destroy it, just like they've destroyed all the other planets they've ever lived on."

I couldn't believe what the professor was telling me. My mind felt like a bullet of information had shattered it into smithereens.

"Why Earth? Why not invade Jupiter, or Mars?" I asked angrily. I didn't want to give up my home for some oversized cat!

"The Partek feel that Earth is the only planet that's worth taking," Professor Andrews explained. "That's why their fleet of spaceships has been hovering dangerously close to Earth for weeks. They're getting ready to attack any day."

"And the Partek are roaming the Earth disguised as cats?" I asked.

"Not exactly," said Dr Burden. "They're using the cats on Earth to help them."

"How? There must be a way we can stop them," I said.

"We've told you enough," said Dr Burden.

"Yes," agreed Professor Andrews. "Stay here while we report to Captain Drake."

Without another word, they left the room and locked the door behind them.

I sat back, trying to make sense of everything they'd just told me. Feeling something poking my fingers, I quickly stood up. I turned the chair upside down and found an envelope with my name on it. I ripped it open.

WHAT DO YOU GET IF YOU CROSS A PARTEK WITH A SNOWMAN?

FROSTBITE!

FIND A PARTEK AND ASK IT THESE QUESTIONS:

WHAT'S THE MOST FASCINATING HUMAN INVENTION?

1. WHAT'S THE MOST IMPORTANT PART OF A CAT?
2. WHAT'S THE MOST IMPORTANT PART OF A CAT?
3. WHY USE FOOT SOLDIERS?

MORPH HAS A COMPUTER PROGRAM.

THE DARE SATELLITE HAS A COMPUTER SYSTEM.

THEY HAVE A PASSWORD. HERE'S A CLUE.

- .... . | -... .. --. --. . ... - | ... .- .-. -.- |

..--..

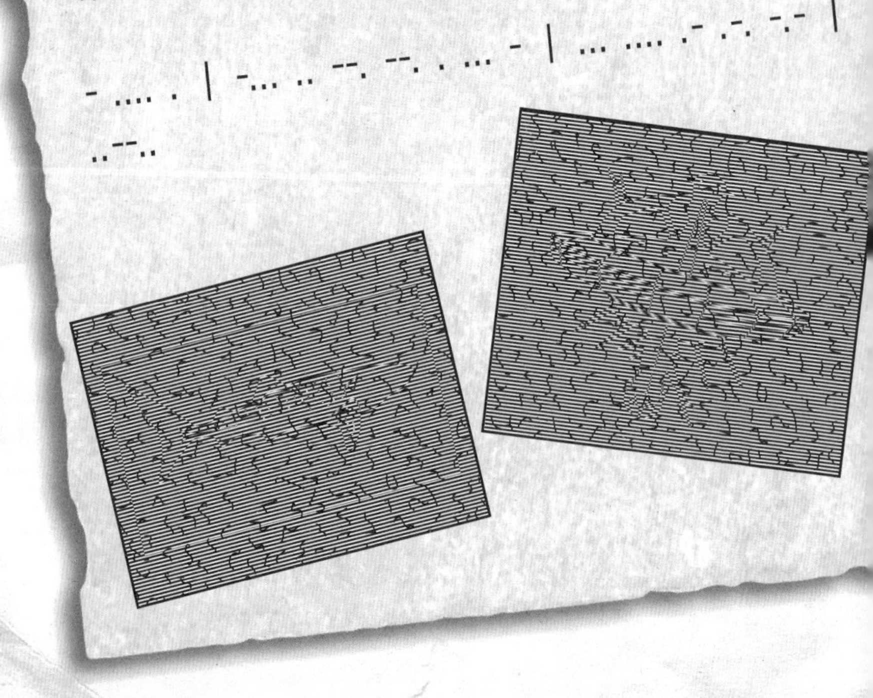

I quickly translated the Morse code on my SurfM8:

THE BIGGEST SHARK?

I didn't need to look up what the biggest shark was – I already knew.

The biggest shark = the Whale Shark.

I quickly fumbled through my bag and pulled out Morph. Pressing my thumb down on the keypad, I activated the tiny spaceship and turned it into a computer.

Sure enough, I found the DARE Satellite computer system and tapped in the password: whale shark.

Success!

I clicked on the link marked PARTEK, and this is what I found.

Name: Partek
Home Planet: Partek (extinct), Zeno galaxy.
Biology: Related to cats in the same way that humans are related to apes.
Known: Partek can communicate with Earthling cats - means unknown...

Everything was slotting together like the pieces of a puzzle.

The Partek were communicating with the cats on Earth, but how? I needed to come face-to-face with a Partek and ask it the questions in my letter.

Just then the door swung open and Professor Andrews walked in.

I shoved Morph and my SurfM8 into my bag as quickly as I could.

He marched towards me with a grim look on his face and started to speak. "I've been instructed to take you to the prison deck until further notice."

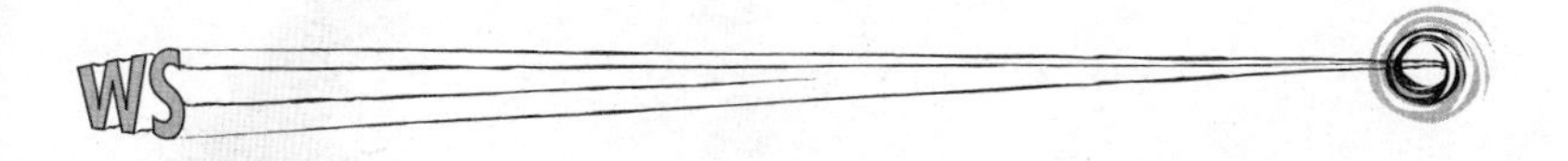

I struggled to escape Professor Andrews's grasp on my wrist. "You have to listen to me!" I shouted at him. "I really am here to help you!"

But he wouldn't listen to a word I said.

I was led into room five on the Hume Deck. It was just like room three – full of frozen Partek.

"You're going to freeze me?" I shouted in shock.

"No, I'm going to ask you to stay in this room where we can monitor you," he said, pointing to a surveillance camera on the wall.

I started to head for the door.

"You're not leaving," Professor Andrews

shouted. He pulled on my shoulder and spun me around. My backpack flew out of my hands and hit one of the freezer doors.

The door cracked down the middle and the sound of shattering ice filled the room.

"Now look what you've done!" Professor Andrews gasped. "You've smashed one of the freezers – the Partek will escape!"

"I need to speak to it," I said calmly.

"Are you insane?" he said, laughing in panic.

"No," I replied. "I've got a job to do."

I walked towards the door, lifted out my amulet, and pressed it against the lock. The door clicked shut – we were locked in. I couldn't risk letting the Partek escape.

I heard a sinister purr coming from the freezer.

"Stand back," I warned Professor Andrews.

The Partek leaped from the freezer, changing

from cat to beast in midair.

I whipped the stun gun from my bag and shot a small blast at it. The beast fell to the floor with a groan and started to writhe around in pain.

The Partek started to growl at me. It bared its teeth and the claws of its scaly arm started to poke out of its mouth.

"I'm going to ask you three questions," I said to the Partek as calmly as I could. "If you answer them, I won't hurt you. First, what's the most fascinating human invention?"

"Radio," the Partek answered.

"And what's the most important part of a cat?"

"Whissskers," the Partek hissed.

"Why foot soldiers?" I asked.

"Cannot land until humansss are dead," the Partek answered.

The scientists outside started banging on the

door. The Partek hissed and spat. It began to slink towards me on its giant paws.

"Oh, no, you don't," I said as I shot him with a stunning blast from my gun.

The Partek screeched in pain.

"Will, what were you asking?" Professor Andrews mumbled.

"Don't you see?" I said. "The Partek are sending radio signals to Earth that are being picked up by cats. Their whiskers act as some kind of antennae. The radio signals must be instructing the cats to prepare for the invasion. It's telling them to kill everyone on Earth because the Partek can't land until everyone's dead."

Out of nowhere, the Partek let out the most incredible roar I'd ever heard. I covered my ears and felt my face ripple with the force of the roar. Behind the terrible screeching I heard the sound of smashing glass.

Professor Andrews ran for the door and I followed. One press of the amulet and the door clicked open.

"Explain to the others what's going on," I instructed Professor Andrews.

I pulled out my SurfM8 and quickly IM'd Zoe – I had to let her know about the cats on Earth.

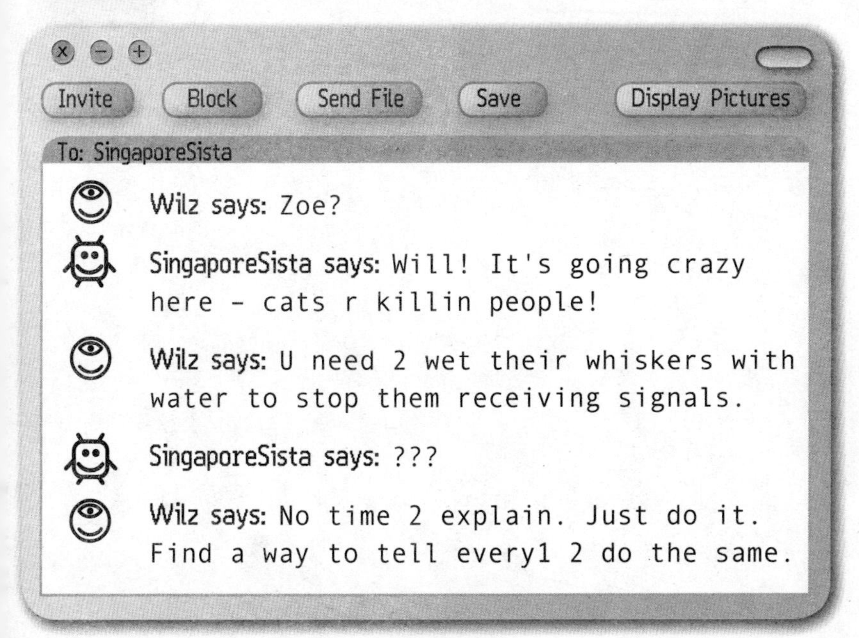

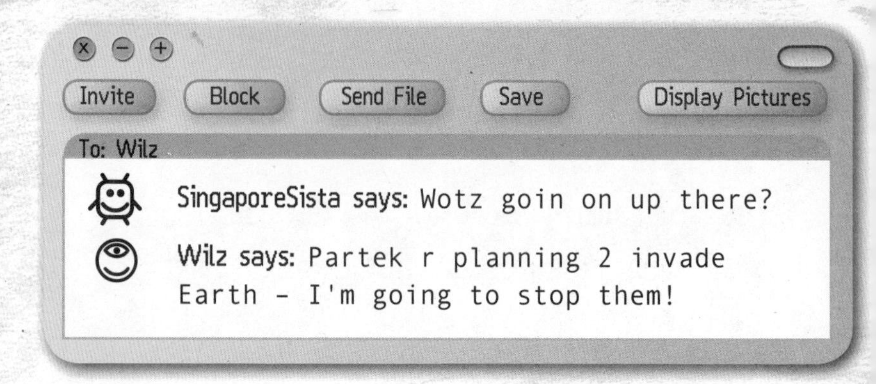

I shoved the SurfM8 back into my pocket and looked up in horror. Every door on the corridor was creaking open to reveal flaming Partek eyes. The roar had been so loud it had cracked the frozen cages of every Partek on the satellite…

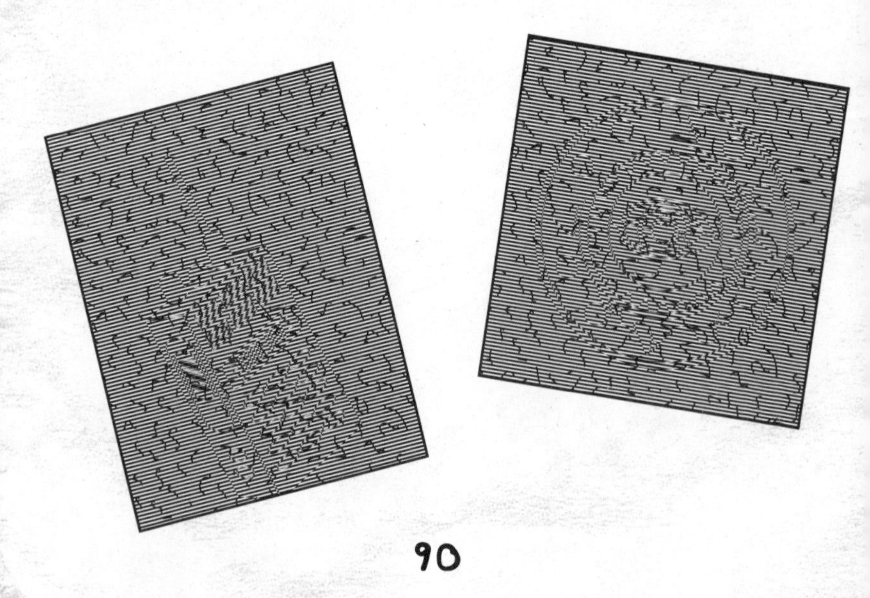

CHAPTER EIGHT
PARTEK ATTACK

The Partek prowled into the satellite corridor and purred in threatening tones. One of the nearby scientists grabbed his radio and pressed down on the receiver.

"Code red! Repeat, code red," he said, trembling.

The radio crackled and a voice boomed, "Affirmative. Captain Drake is on his way."

Terrified screams and panicked voices filled the air. Scientists started to run in every direction, tripping over each other as they went.

A jet-black Partek paced over to Professor Andrews and let out a menacing snarl. Its lips parted and its clawed hand clamped around Professor Andrews's neck, squeezing tightly. The Partek lifted him off the ground and his legs kicked in the air. His face was a deep shade of red and his eyes were bulging from his head.

"Help... me!" he managed to choke.

I blasted the giant cat with my stun gun and it dropped Professor Andrews in an instant.

Another Partek let out a ferocious roar. We all covered our ears.

There was chaos everywhere. I felt hot breath on my neck and slowly turned around...

An angry Partek was standing right behind me. I reached for my stun gun, but another Partek knocked it from my hands. I reached into my bag and pulled out Dad's Supersonic Screecher, blasting it at full volume. The noise was so loud that some of the scientists fainted. I had a split second to reach for my stun gun. Running down the corridor, I blasted as many Partek as I could.

With a stun gun in one hand and the Screecher in the other, I let rip. The Partek started to shrink into tiny cats as I blasted them.

"Lock up the kittens!" I called to Professor Andrews. All I could think about was trying to obliterate the Partek.

"There's no time, Will! Follow me!" Professor Andrews shouted.

I ran towards him, my stun gun at the ready. We dodged our way past the Partek and I stunned a couple for good measure.

"Take that, you oversized alley cats!" I shouted as they fell to the floor and shrank into kittens.

Professor Andrews led me away from the chaos and into a room on a quieter corridor. He turned and looked me in the eye. "Will," he began, "I'm sorry I didn't believe you when you said you were Henry's son. The truth is, we need you now – everyone on planet Earth needs you. Your father invented a defence shield that could protect the Earth from Partek invasion. The problem is, your dad is the only person who knows the code word to activate that shield."

"OK..." I said.

"There's more," Professor Andrews continued. "The shield is made of kelp dust, which contains a chemical that is toxic to the Partek. Once activated, the shield will act like a brick wall around the Earth and the Partek will have no way to invade. The shield must be activated at a location about two hundred miles from here."

"Easy," I said. "My spaceship can cover that distance in minutes."

"The location is infested with Partek spacecraft.

It's a suicide mission, Will."

"I'll be OK," I assured him. "Trust me, I'm an Adventurer. All I have to do is blast into space and fight my way through a fleet of Partek spaceships until I get to the location. Then I just type the code word into the DARE computer system and the shield will be activated. Simple."

Professor Andrews looked over his shoulder nervously.

"You need to leave the satellite without anyone knowing – otherwise Captain Drake will try to stop you. The reason I took you to this room is that it's not bugged. Look above you..."

I looked up. The ceiling was panelled.

"Above those panels is a shaft. I'm going to help you get up there and you're going to have to crawl your way through the shaft. You need to go all the way to the end, turn right, take the third left, fourth right, fifth right and then jump down the chute. That will take you to the shuttle bay."

Professor Andrews took a small notebook and pen from his coat pocket and scribbled something on a piece of paper. "These are the coordinates of the activation location."

I put the piece of paper in my pocket and Professor Andrews lifted me up to push one of the ceiling tiles. Sure enough, it moved. I climbed up.

The shaft was narrow, and I had to crawl. I made my way to the end and took a right turn. Then I took the third left, the fourth right after that, then the fifth right... Then I jumped into the chute. I landed in a deserted docking bay and pulled Morph out of my bag. I activated the spaceship program and watched it pop up in front of me, then climbed in and entered the coordinates.

The satellite doors opened and Morph glided out into space. I knew where I was going, but had no idea how I was going to deal with the Partek when I got there. Back with Professor Andrews I'd been so confident about cracking the code. But how was I actually going to find the word to activate the defence shield and save the world? At that moment it seemed an impossible task...

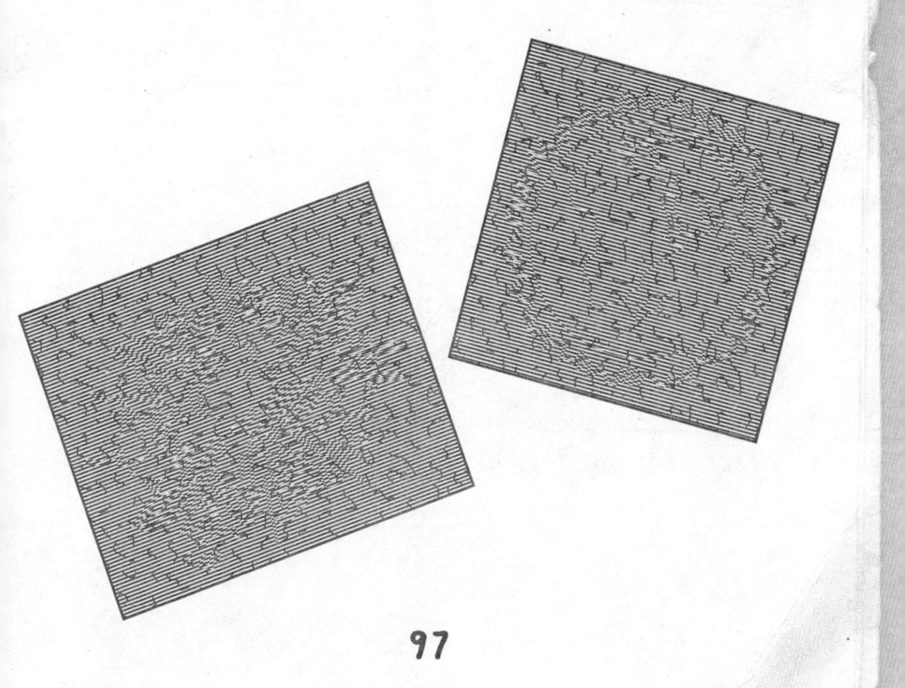

CHAPTER NINE
CRACKING THE CODE

Morph started cruising at about 1,000 mph – at this rate I'd be in Partek-infested space within a matter of minutes.

I didn't have much time to work out the code. I knew my dad better than any of those scientists did – trying to come up with a word that only he would think of should have been easy, but it wasn't. I racked my brains, but nothing seemed right.

Quickly I searched the spaceship for envelopes, but couldn't find any. Then a thought struck me like a bolt of lightning – I still hadn't translated the code on the first letter I'd found on the satellite! Why hadn't I thought of that sooner?

Pulling the letter out of my pocket, I switched on my SurfM8 and typed the code into the translator. It only took a couple of seconds to translate:

Fish beginning with K, 7 letters

Fish that began with the letter K and had seven letters… I knew the answer! It seemed so obvious – not just Grandpa Monty's favourite food, but Dad's too!

An IM message popped up on the screen.

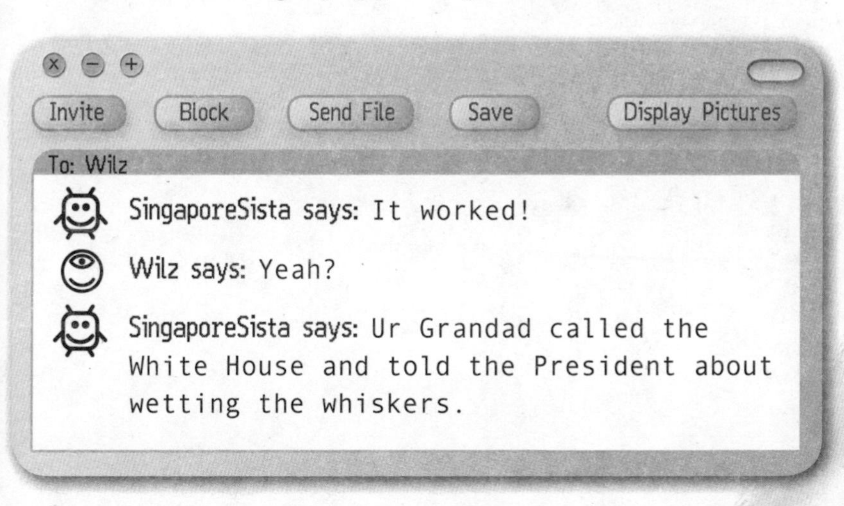

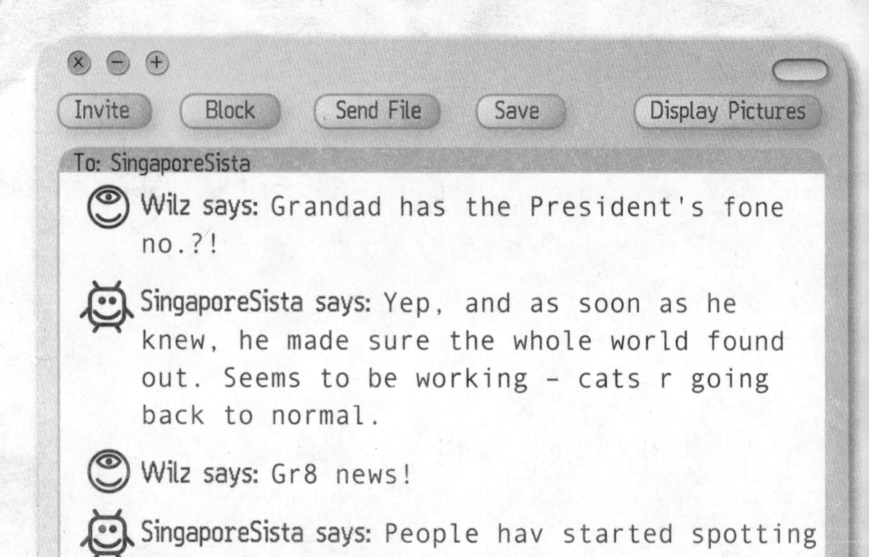

I didn't get a chance to IM her back. Something hit Morph with a force more powerful than a hurricane.

BANG!

A second hit swiped the side of the spacecraft and threw me to the floor.

Partek spaceships surrounded us on every side. Every one of the alien ships was flying in the same direction – towards Earth!

CRASH!

I felt another rocket torpedo through space and smash into Morph. The Partek knew I'd come to fight them and were attacking me with everything they had.

I looked at Morph's control deck and scanned it for some kind of rocket launcher. Found it! I pressed down on the button and instantly a huge missile was flying away from Morph and towards a Partek spaceship. The rocket collided with the ship and blew it to smithereens. Awesome!

"Yes!" I shouted triumphantly, punching the air.

I was too quick to celebrate – an alien rocket zoomed towards me, narrowly missing Morph.

"Close, cat-face, but not close enough!" I

screamed with anger.

I pressed the button that said 'Gun' and waited to start spluttering bullets into space – but that's not what happened. A panel in Morph's control deck flipped back and a steering wheel rose up. This wasn't just any gun – it was a laser gun, like the ones in computer games.

I took hold of the laser gun steering wheel with a smile on my face.

"Hey pussycats," I shouted at the top of my voice, "what do you get when you cross the Partek with an Adventure? Fireworks!"

I pointed the laser gun at a Partek spaceship and fired... BOOM!

Laser gunfire catapulted through space and obliterated the Partek battleships.

The Partek were soaring towards Earth at super speed. As they travelled they fired everything they had in my direction. Morph dodged the alien bullets while somehow managing to keep on course – I had to travel to where I could activate the defence shield!

I kept a tight hold on the gun and directed it to the Partek spacecraft that were soaring through the skies. My fingers kept hold of the trigger as I fired left and right and took down the spaceships one by one.

My eyes were darting between the battle and Morph's GPS system. I didn't have far to go before I could activate Dad's defence shield… CRASH!

Morph shook from side to side and a worrying whizzing noise started to roar from the spaceship motor. Morph's lights started to flicker and dim.

"Not now!" I shouted. If Morph broke down in space I'd have no hope of survival – and Earth would have no hope of being saved!

Aaarrgghhhh!

I launched more missiles to strike the Partek ships.
Morph's radar told me I was almost in position to activate the shield.
I hacked into the DARE Satellite computer system, navigated my way to the defence shield page, and typed in 'KIPPERS'.
ACTIVATE
Then I pressed one last button...

Silence. The Partek had stopped firing at me. But I could still see the menacing lights of their fleet zooming in Earth's direction. Had it worked?

Suddenly the view outside the windows changed. One by one, the lights went out and there was complete darkness.

Then something really weird happened. Morph started to shake as if it had been caught up in a hurricane. The computer monitors went crazy and started bleeping over and over. Suddenly thousands of Partek spaceships flew past the window. They were flying away from Earth this time, not towards it. It was as if someone had put all the spaceships in a giant catapult and fired them as far away from Earth as they could.

Dad's force field was working! It was repelling the Partek!

Suddenly the sound of silence was interrupted

Woo hoo!

by the crackling of Morph's radio.

"Will? Come in, Will?" It was Professor Andrews. "Will, are you there? The defence shield has been activated. You've done it – you've saved Earth! The Partek are retreating!"

Relief swept over me – Earth was safe! And it felt pretty good to be the person who had saved it.

Morph made a spluttering sound and jolted from side to side.

"My ship's been damaged," I shouted into the receiver.

"Head back to the DARE Satellite," Professor Andrews said over the radio. "Our engineers will fix it."

All I wanted to do was go back home and make sure everyone on Earth was OK, but I knew Morph wouldn't make it. So, slowly, I steered

Morph in a 180-degree turn and began travelling back to the satellite.

Morph's radio started to crackle and buzz again. I looked down at the control panel and saw that the GPS monitor had clouded over with static. How was I going to find my way back to the satellite without a GPS system?

But getting back to the ship was the least of my worries.

A shape started to appear through the fuzz on the computer screen – the face of a giant cat.

"Will Solvit!" boomed a voice over Morph's radio. It definitely wasn't Professor Andrews this time; there was nothing human about it.

"Yes," I said calmly. I wasn't going to be scared by an alien that I'd just fought out of the skies.

"Earth may be safe for now, but we will be back, and it will take more than you to stop us."

How does it know about my dad?

I sighed. Earth was safe – for now.

But then the voice said something that I've thought about every day since – a few words that have been echoing in my mind over and over, haunting me.

The voice said: "Your father is somewhere you will never find him."

?

Then that was it – gone. Morph's computer screen clouded over and the Partek face disappeared.

I pressed down on the radio button again, "What? What?" I wanted to know what he meant. But all I could hear was the sound of radio static.

The GPS system reactivated itself and started directing me back to the satellite.

I let go of the steering wheel and put Morph on autopilot. I was only a few minutes away from the satellite, but I didn't care. All I wanted was a chance to come face to face with the Partek again.

'Your father is somewhere you will never find him.' What did that mean?

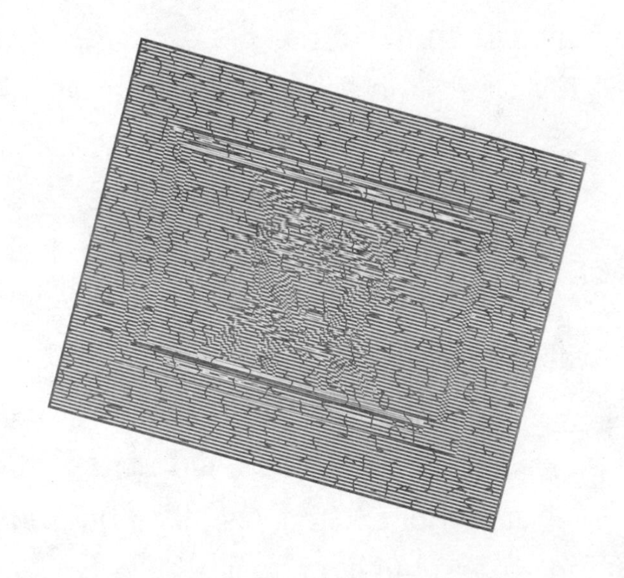

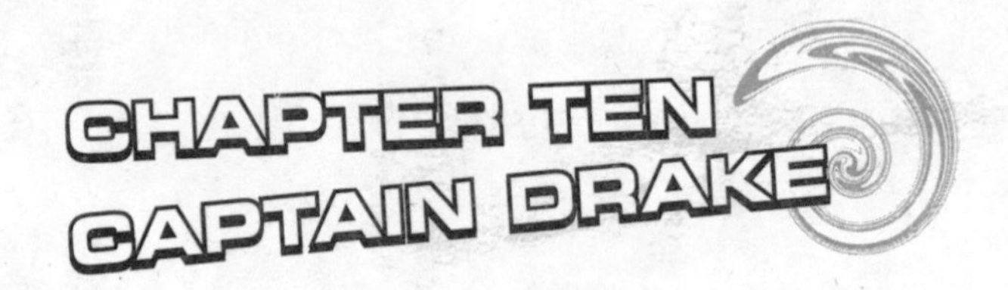

CHAPTER TEN CAPTAIN DRAKE

I repeated the words over and over in my head. Why would the Partek say that to me? Who could I ask for help? Who would understand?

I was too busy thinking to notice Morph chugging into the DARE Satellite's docking bay. Before I knew it, there was a group of scientists waiting outside for me.

"Will!" shouted Professor Andrews as Morph's spaceship doors opened and I climbed out.

A crowd of excited scientists bustled around me and started talking at once.

"How did you know the defence shield code word?" one man asked.

"You saved the world!" another man cried.

A woman picked me up and hugged me.

"Is it over?" I asked Professor Andrews.

He nodded. "Yes – thanks to Henry's force field and your quick thinking. Now all we have to do is be ready if the Partek come back."

"So Earth's not really safe?" I asked.

"It is for now, but not indefinitely. You've bought us some time, though. We owe you a lot, Will. If there's anything we can do to help you...."

"Well, there is my spaceship," I said. "Morph took a serious beating."

"Leave it to us," he said, grinning.

A group of men wearing blue overalls and carrying toolboxes made their way towards Morph.

"I'm going to take you to meet Captain Drake," Professor Andrews told me, smiling.

He led me down a flight of stairs and into a lift

shaft. He pressed a button that said 'Control Deck' and the lift started to move. When the lift doors opened, we were in front of another set of doors with a lock. Professor Andrews pulled out an amulet just like mine.

"Professor Andrews," I began, "what does the symbol on the amulet mean?"

But before he had a chance to answer me, the doors swooshed open to reveal a huge room crowded with people. They stopped what they were doing and looked at me.

"I've brought the Adventurer," Professor Andrews said as we walked inside.

"Aha," said one man, smiling. As we walked closer to him I saw that he was wearing a name tag saying 'Captain Drake'. He shook my hand and everyone in the control room clapped.

"My name's Will," I said to Captain Drake.

"Will Solvit."

Captain Drake was taller than anyone I'd ever met before. He had big, bushy eyebrows and a nose that looked like he'd been in a few fights during his life.

"I knew your father," Captain Drake said to me quietly, so no one else could hear. "We went to school together."

"He's missing," I told him.

"I wondered why I hadn't heard from him." Captain Drake looked thoughtful. "It would be unlike Henry to stay quiet when the Earth's in danger. He always loved a good Partek fight!"

I didn't know what to say. There were so many things I wanted to ask Captain Drake, like if he knew where my dad was, and how long he and Dad had known about the Partek. But everyone in the room was looking at me and I didn't want them to hear.

"I have something to give you, Will," Captain Drake said.

Dr Burden walked over to the captain, holding a small brown box that she passed to him.

Captain Drake opened the box and pulled out a shiny gold medal. It wasn't the kind of medal you hang around your neck – not like my amulet or the medals that people get when they win a race. It was the kind of medal that you pin to a jacket – like the ones soldiers wear.

"It's the DARE Medal of Honour," he told me as he pinned it to my T-shirt.

"Thanks," I said, grinning.

No big deal!

"Thank you for your help today, Will," Captain Drake said to me. "If it weren't for you, Earth would have been doomed."

"No problem," I replied. "I'm just doing what Adventurers are supposed to do. No big deal really."

Captain Drake smiled at me and tipped his cap. "Spoken like a true Adventurer," he said.

I stayed and talked to Captain Drake and the other scientists for ages. They wanted to know how I knew the code word and how a ten-year-old had a spaceship – I told them what I could, but obviously had to keep most of it secret.

I noticed that Captain Drake kept smiling to himself whenever I avoided telling people about the letters I got. I wondered if he knew that Dad had gotten letters when he was younger. I wondered if Captain Drake had been with Dad on any of his Adventures.

At long last, Professor Andrews came and tapped me on the shoulder. "Your spaceship is fixed and ready," he told me.

That was the best news I'd heard all day! All I wanted to do was get home to Solvit Hall.

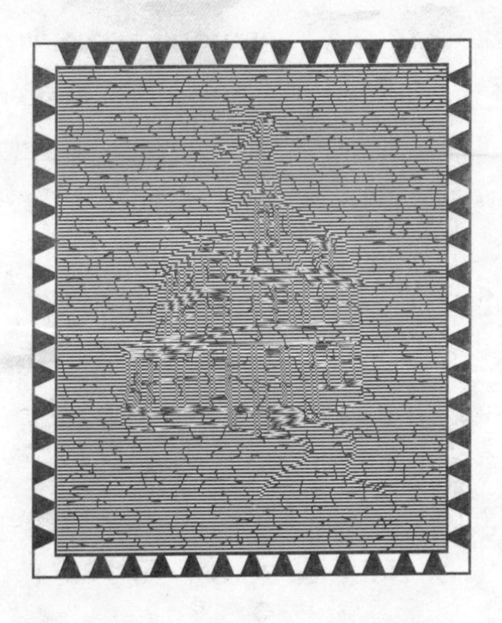

After I'd said goodbye to everyone, I went to talk to Captain Drake. I quickly told him what the Partek had said about my dad.

"Leave it to me," he whispered. "I'll see what I can do."

I said goodbye to Professor Andrews, Dr Burden, and the others, then climbed into Morph and shut the door behind me.

I strapped myself in and revved up Morph's engine, then backed out of the docking bay. The scientists outside were all waving and shouting things like 'Good luck' and 'Come back soon'.

Before I knew it, Morph had left the satellite

and was blasting through space.

I took out my home-pointing compass and held it up to Morph's navigation system. I programmed in a route back to Grandpa's garden and hit the button that said 'Autopilot'.

The spaceship went into freefall and I took off my belt and started to float around.

I watched the solar system zoom past the window and thought about everything that had happened…

There was still so much I didn't know – like when the Partek might try to invade Earth again, and whether I was ever going to see my parents.

I took Grandpa's diary out of my bag, opened it at random, and read the first entry I could find.

Coooooool!!

30th September 1957

I'll never forget my first Adventure. After following a trail of clues left for me in letters, I found myself in Alaska. I rode on the back of a whale, fought a bear, and spent three months living with an Inuit family. At times it was terrifying and at other times I thought I would never be happier.

I remember coming home and thinking that life would suddenly go back to normal. It never did. When one Adventure ends, another begins. That's what life is, one big Adventure.

I knew that Grandpa was right – life would be nothing but crazy adventures from now on. Reading Grandpa's diary made being an Adventurer feel easier – I felt like I wasn't alone, like I was part of something special.

Soon Earth came into view. We got closer and closer and started to slow down as we entered the Earth's atmosphere.

I saw the shape of the United States.

Then I saw my home state. Then I could see the town I lived in.

Soon I could see Solvit Hall.

Morph landed with a bump in the backyard.

Grandpa, Zoe, and Plato were there waiting. They rushed towards me as I opened the spaceship door.

"You're alive!" cried Zoe. "Grandpa Monty told me everything..."

"Good job, son," said Grandpa Monty.

I turned Morph off and it shrank into a pocket-sized spaceship.

"So much has happened," said Zoe. "The sky filled up with spaceships... the President said we were heading for an intergalactic war... and..."

Zoe wouldn't stop talking – she wanted to tell me everything that had gone on while I was in space. Apparently the sky was so jam-packed with Partek ships, you couldn't even see the sun. She told me about the cats going crazy and how they chilled out when their whiskers were made wet. Then she told me how all of the Partek spaceships had suddenly zoomed back up into space.

I told them all about the DARE Satellite and the Partek spaceships waiting to invade Earth. I told them about Captain Drake and Professor Andrews and Dr Burden and about how the Partek could

Stinky!

communicate with cats. And I told them how I stopped the invasion by activating Dad's force field.

When I finished I waited for one of them to speak.

"Peanut butter and jam sandwich?" asked Grandpa. "Or maybe some kippers?" he said with a wink.

Plato yapped approvingly.

"Honestly, Will," Zoe said, "this is all just so… so… unbelievable! You saved the world! Do you know what that means?"

I thought about it for a moment as Grandpa passed me one of his famous peanut butter and jam sandwiches. It was pretty cool. But no way was I letting on to her that I was proud of myself. "It doesn't mean anything," I said nonchalantly, taking a humongous bite out of my sandwich.

After a while, Zoe's mum came to pick her up.

"Don't worry," Zoe whispered as she was walking out of the front door. "Your secret's safe with me."

"I know," I yawned. I was so tired. Saving the Earth was really hard work.

I said goodnight to Grandpa and headed up to bed. I dragged my feet up the winding staircase, past the portraits of all the Adventurers who had lived before me. Dad's picture was right at the end. I wished so much that my dad had been there that day – not because I needed him to help me, but because I wanted him to tell me I'd done a good job.

I opened my bedroom door. There was an envelope addressed to me sitting on my bed. My heart skipped a beat – another Adventure already? I sat on my bed and opened the letter, nervous about what it might say.

WHERE DO ASTRONAUTS LEAVE THEIR SPACESHIPS?

AT PARKING METEORS!

CONGRATULATIONS ON TODAY – YOU DID AN EXCELLENT JOB. THE EARTH IS SAFE AGAIN BECAUSE OF YOU. BUT THIS IS ONLY THE BEGINNING, WILL. THE EARTH IS NEVER SAFE FOR LONG – THERE WILL ALWAYS BE ADVENTURES TO GO ON, CODES TO CRACK, AND BATTLES TO FIGHT.

THIS IS YOUR DESTINY, WILL.

YOUR PARENTS WERE PROUD OF YOU TODAY.

What? How could my parents be proud of me? They were stuck in a prehistoric jungle, weren't they?

Who was sending the letters? Was I ever going

to find out what my Adventurer skill really was, or what had really happened to Mum and Dad that day in the jungle?

If only I could talk to my parents, maybe everything else would fall into place. There was only one way I was going to do that – I had to go back in time.

I took Morph out of my pocket and stared at it. I knew right there and then what my next Adventure would be. I was going to find a way to go back in time, no matter what.

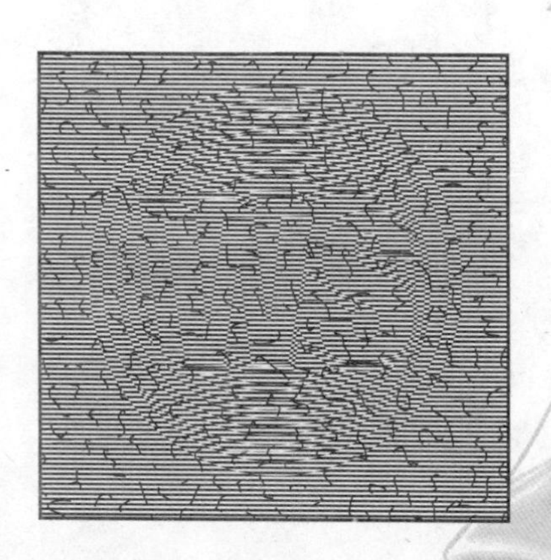

WILL SOLVIT
AND THE MUMMY'S CURSE
A zombie mummy reached its blackened fingernails towards me and ripped at my T-shirt.
Untie him, stinky bones!

Tiy threw me a spear and we started fighting the mummies. It wasn't working – we were outnumbered!
We're mummy food!
Then I remembered the last line of my letter...
Grabbing the mirror from my pocket, I held it up to the nearest mummy. His eyes burst in his head and his body caught fire.
The adventure continues...

OTHER BOOKS IN THE SERIES